DEATH IN THE OPENING CHAPTER

DEATH IN THE OPENING CHAPTER

Tim Heald

CRÈME de la CRIME

This first world edition published 2011
in Great Britain and the USA by
Crème de la Crime, an imprint of
SEVERN HOUSE PUBLISHERS LTD of
9–15 High Street, Sutton, Surrey, England, SM1 1DF.
Trade paperback edition first published
in Great Britain and the USA 2011.

British Library Cataloguing in Publication Data

Heald, Tim.
    Death in the opening chapter. – (Simon Bognor mysteries)
    1. Bognor, Simon (Fictitious character) – Fiction.
    2. Government investigators – Fiction. 3. Clergy – Crimes
    against – Fiction. 4. Detective and mystery stories.
    I. Title II. Series
    823.9'14-dc22

ISBN-13: 978-1-78029-002-7 (cased)
ISBN-13: 978-1-78029-502-2 (trade paper)

All Severn House titles are printed on acid-free paper.

Severn House Publishers support The Forest Stewardship Council [FSC],
the leading international forest certification organisation. All our titles that
are printed on Greenpeace-approved FSC-certified paper carry the FSC logo.

MIX
Paper from
responsible sources
FSC
www.fsc.org   FSC® C018575

Typeset by Palimpsest Book Production Ltd.,
Falkirk, Stirlingshire, Scotland.
Printed and bound in Great Britain by the
MPG Books Group, Bodmin, Cornwall.

*For Kits and Hacker, who provided the original idea,
and for Graeme and Pip, Robyn and David,
who provided peace and quiet, not to mention
inspirational views.*

ONE

The Reverend Sebastian Fludd unlocked the door to his church, walked up the aisle, crossed himself, knelt briefly in prayer and then sat down in one of the front pews. Such was his wont as he began to think about tomorrow's sermon. It was one of the most important of the year – less so than Christmas or Easter, but more significant than any other – for it heralded the annual Flanagan Fludd Literary Festival, which had been held for a decade in the pretty little seaside town of Mallborne.

The Reverend Sebastian was descended, vaguely, from the eponymous festival dedicatee and his presence as vicar of the small but perfectly formed thirteenth-century Saint Teath's church owed something to this and to the presence in the decaying manor house of Sir Branwell Fludd, the fourteenth baronet, who, being the great grandson of the poet, pageant-contriver and pantomime-composer after whom the festival was named, was even more closely connected with the festival than his distant cousin, the rector. His living was, in effect, under Sir Branwell's control. However, the bishop, something of a radical (though described by some as a closet conservative), was inclined to dispute this feudal relic.

Much of Mallborne was still under the control of Sir Branwell and Lady Fludd, for the town had, on the whole, resisted New Labour and such novel concepts as democracy and progress. The Fludd cousins and the rest of the community behaved as if nothing of any great significance had happened in Mallborne for the last thousand or so years. In this, they might have seemed unfashionable, but they were also, more or less, correct.

Sebastian opened his Bible and read, sotto voce, 'In the beginning was the word.'

The Gospel according to St John, Chapter One, beginning

at the first verse. Just the ticket for a literary festival. 'And the word was God. And the word was with God.' Strange that he had never used this text before. He believed that the King James Bible was one of the great works of English literature, that the words in it were beautiful and beautifully arranged. They were, in a very real sense, the words of God and this would be the theme of his talk from the pulpit this Sunday. God knows what the words meant but that was not unusual when it came to the Bible, or anything else. Perhaps that would be his theme: an exasperated shrug and spreading of the hands, together with a sighed, 'God knows!'

Faith sat lightly on the shoulders of God's servant Sebastian Fludd. In fact, it sat so lightly that its gossamer-like ethereality was often non-existent. He was more of a lugubrious agnostic than a cheerful atheist, but he could not, in all conscience, be described as a conventional believer. He had only taken orders because as the younger son of a younger son it had seemed the right, indeed the only, thing to do.

Truth to tell, he should have done almost anything else, and in a more up-to-date family he might have done so. The Fludd family, however, had been sending their problem children into the church since the Reformation and beyond. There were uncommitted Reverend Fludds littering the foot-notes of English history virtually since English history first began. True, there had been the occasional committed fire-brand Fludds, and one had even been burned at the stake for his convictions. On the whole, however, the ecclesiastical Fludds belonged to the Laodicean wing of the church, being neither hot nor cold, and worthy, therefore, of being spewed out by the likes of St Paul, who was made, it went without saying, of sterner stuff.

The Reverend Sebastian was feeling a bit spewed out, himself, that night as he contemplated the Gospel according to St John. Sir Branwell had given him a wigging; Mrs Fludd had done the same and there had been two anonymous letters which were unsettling. And he had had a run-in with the chef-proprietor of the pub – the cook with the funny foreign name. He felt beleaguered. It was no fun being a vicar these days, particularly if you had trouble believing in God, let alone the ludicrous beliefs that went with Him. The Reverend Sebastian had much sympathy with same-sex marriage and the ordination of women as bishops. These relatively progressive views did not find sympathy with either Lady Fludd nor Sir Branwell. Nor was he entirely sure of his Bishop, Ebenezer, nor indeed his wife, Dorcas. Luckily, the Reverend Sebastian did not hold his beliefs very strongly, not being given to strong beliefs about anything much. Which was, perhaps, part of his problem and why, in middle age, he was rector of St Teath's, Mallborne, and likely to remain so for the foreseeable future.

He frowned over the words and concentrated on the Good Book so hard that he did not hear the click of the church door, which he had left unlocked, or the soft pad of footsteps up the aisle.

He enjoyed the literary festival, even though he was sceptical about his ancestor who struck him as a Victorian ranter and charlatan. He had a long white beard like an old-fashioned version of God the Father Almighty and his poetry quite definitely did not stand the test of time, being, in his opinion, ponderous, pompous and unduly orotund. The rhymes, which were frequent, were obvious, as were the sentiments. Never mind, the festival was fun and alliterative. He was sorry they were not having Salman Rushdie whose humour he much enjoyed. For some reason Lady Fludd, who was a sort of de facto literary director of the festival, did not find Rushdie funny, so he went uninvited, which the Reverend Sebastian thought rather a pity.

Some people thought Rushdie's sense of humour about as funny as those old-fashioned 'cartoons' in which the United Kingdom is represented by a man in breeches with a Union Flag as his waistcoat and a bulldog at his feet. This was thought by some London *bien savants* to be genuinely droll, and as far as the Reverend Sebastian was concerned, Rushdie's humour was at the cutting edge. He thought his mace was a rapier. In other words, the vicar had a rudimentary sense of humour. Or possibly none at all. He obviously wouldn't recognize a joke until he had had it explained, by which time it would have lost any point it might once have had. In other words, Rushdie was funny. In this, he was probably in a minority. He also believed Rushdie to be functionally illiterate. His was not a popular view, except in Mallborne, where it was virtually unanimous. In any case, this view had nothing to do with being asked to participate in the local literary festival. Rather the reverse.

He sighed, something he seemed to do with increasing frequency these days. Life, he conceded, had turned out to be a bit of a flop as far as he was concerned. Still, he got hate mail. Not as much as Rushdie, and as far as he knew no fatwa had ever been issued on his behalf. Most of the hate mail was from gays and lesbians, which was a pity and not entirely fair, since the attitudes of which they accused him were not, strictly speaking, his own, but those of Sir Branwell who was, when it came to attitudes and much else besides, his lord and master. Attitudes: Anglo-Saxon. There had been a book with that title once. It was by Angus Wilson, an author whom he much admired, though he was now a forgotten taste and had died before he could be invited to the literary festival.

The Reverend Sebastian had a lot to do with the festival, quite apart from preaching the sermon at the service which always preceded it. He and Lady Fludd tended to choose the speakers, even though the conceit was that power resided with the council. The council was in this, as in most things, a nuisance, but Mallborne was essentially feudal and therefore the council's writ did not really run. The Reverend and Lady Fludd called the shots without a great deal of opposition. Smallwood from the council did most of the work; Sir Branwell and Dorcas, wife of the reverend, heckled half-heartedly, except in the rare instances, such as that of Salman Rushdie, when they had what might reasonably be described as a point of view. But, basically, the Rev. and Her Ladyship did as they wished.

It could be said that the festival put Mallborne on the map, though the map was not, on the whole, somewhere that Mallborne wished to be on. In a sense, the little town – or was it a large village? No one seemed quite sure – was

a bit like him. He did not want to be on a map. He preferred
anonymity. He wanted to pass through life unnoticed. He
didn't even hanker for Andy Warhol's fifteen minutes of
fame. Fame was emphatically for other people, even if it
was only fleeting. One of his favourite passages in literature
– and on the whole he was fond of reading and liked books
– was the end of *The Mayor of Casterbridge* by Thomas
Hardy. Hardy had an epitaph for Michael Henchard which
said simply that he was a good man and did good things.
That was fine by the Reverend Sebastian. He was completely
devoid of conventional ambition; quite happy to be one of
the crowd; forgettable, forgotten. He was neither happy nor
unhappy. He just was. He took refuge in the encomium
pronounced at a monastic funeral service by a former Bishop
of Exeter. 'This was a splendid life,' the bishop had said.
'Splendid in its obscurity and humility; splendid in its
strength and charity; splendid in its achievements.' He sometimes wished he felt stronger and more splendid, but he
nonetheless drew comfort from the late bishop's half-
forgotten words. Blessed, after all, were the meek. And
meek he most certainly was. And even if people like him
were to inherit the earth, that was certainly not his expect-
ation – or even aspiration.

He was musing thus while poring over the Book of
Revelation, when he became aware of a presence. There
was a person in the church with him. Had he been of a
more conventionally religious disposition, he would have
assumed that it was some manifestation of his Lord and
Master: God the Son, God the Father, or God the Holy
Ghost. Or the parish's elusive, not to say shadowy or even
fictional, patron saint. Not given to belief in the supernatural
and being of a naturally sceptical and prosaic disposition,
he presumed that the other person in the church was a human
being who had come in by the open door.

In this he was correct, but what precisely happened in
the next moments, and who precisely the intruder was, is
something that will have to wait for a couple of hundred
pages or so. That is the essence of the mystery, cosy or
'noir'. One begins with a death caused by a person or persons

unknown, for reasons which are similar. The process of unravelling is what gives this sort of story its being, its *raison d'être*.

In the beginning was the corpse and in this case it was the vicar of Mallborne, an inoffensive enough soul, one would have thought. It was his wife, Dorcas, who found him hanging from a rope, which might possibly have done duty in the belfry were it not for the fact that it was suspending the Reverend Sebastian Fludd. Near his feet, which were not more than a few inches above the granite floor of the nave, was a stool that the cleric might conceivably have kicked over himself. If, that is, his death was a suicide; which, though not something one should ever rule out, seemed to the investigating authorities, and even more to the investigating non-authority, to be an unlikely contingency.

The supposition of those who had an interest in the matter was that the Reverend Fludd had been disturbed while contemplating his sermon for the following Sunday, the opening event of the literary festival which he so much enjoyed. The disturbance had been effected by a person unknown to those who came upon the scene later, but, if the lack of apparent struggle was anything to go by, was most probably known to the vicar.

Unfortunately, the priest was one person who no one, save possibly the Almighty, was in a position to question. He would have made an admirable witness, but he was in no position to give evidence, being himself the deceased and therefore the catalyst for the tale which follows. This was, in a sense, rather a splendid death – sudden, unexplained, mysterious; much more tantalizing than the life which had preceded it. Even the Reverend Sebastian Fludd would have found it intriguing. He rather enjoyed a good old-fashioned mystery; preferably a Penguin paperback with a green jacket, and a beginning, a middle and an end. The first tantalizing, the second absorbing and the third unexpected but ultimately reassuring.

Alas, however, this was one mystery that the Reverend Sebastian was not going to enjoy solving, even from the depths of his postprandial, fireside chair, smoking his noxious-smelling pipe as he turned the pages enthusiastically.

This was a murder in which the Reverend Sebastian was an important, but sadly silent, witness.

He was, of course, extremely dead.

TWO

Simon Bognor slapped a generous dollop of farmhouse butter on his wholemeal doorstep of toast, stifled a yawn and helped himself to an equally generous spoonful of chunky home-made marmalade purchased by his hostess at the annual Mallborne fête. He ignored his wife's hostile stare, which combined incredulity and concern in more or less equal measure. Lady Bognor said nothing. Neither Sir Branwell nor Lady Fludd noticed. Or they were too well-bred to comment.

Lady Fludd was reading the *Daily Mail*; Sir Branwell *The Times*. The Bognors were toying with different sections of the *Guardian*. Their choice of breakfast reading spoke volumes but did not tell the whole story.

Bognor and Sir Branwell had been at Apocrypha College, Oxford, together and had become, more or less, chums. They were both, at breakfast that morning, wearing the tie. It was striped, lurid and conveyed a message to the increasingly small number of people who understood the sartorial codes that were once a ubiquitous lingua franca in what passed for the British Establishment. You used to know a man by his necktie, but nowadays it was rare to find one wearing one. Outside, birds sang, mainly seagulls. The Bognors found them charming; the Fludds less so. Familiarity in the avian sense bore hatred rather than mere contempt. The Fludds hated gulls which, more or less surreptitiously, Sir Branwell shot with a .22 he kept by his bed.

The Bognors enjoyed lazy weekends such as this. They reminded them of their past when marmalade had been marmalade and the *Sunday Times* was a proper newspaper. In old age, they had become as grumpy as others of their generation. Tiresomely so at times. It was a tendency of which they were both aware and of which they were tactfully ashamed when in mixed company, which is to say with people younger than themselves. It was not often nowadays that they found themselves with people who were older.

'No deaths worth talking about,' said Bognor through toast and gritted teeth. 'A rock drummer who took an overdose and a very old Professor of Greek from the other place.' In later age, he found himself turning to the obituaries before almost everything else in the paper. It was common among members of his generation.

'Not many dead in *The Times* either,' said Sir Branwell. 'A suffragan bishop and a rather dim sounding major general.'

'And no one dead in the *Daily Mail* at all,' said his wife. 'The *Mail* tends not to do death. Too, too depressing.' She smiled winsomely and asked if anyone wanted more coffee. The cafetière circulated and silence, muffled by munching, descended once more.

'Cow stuck on beach in the *Guardian*,' said Bognor, through toast. 'Must have been a very slow day for a cow stuck on beach to make the *Guardian*.'

'Oh, I don't know,' said his host, genially, 'cows stuck on beaches seem grist to the *Guardian* mill. Ecologically sound. Presumably we are all on the side of the cow? Does George Monbiot have a view on cows? Or Simon Jenkins?'

'I don't think you could run an anti-cow piece in the *Guardian*,' said Monica.

'Unless,' said her husband, 'they'd been cloned or genetically modified in some way. I mean, if the cow stuck on the beach could be shown to be some sort of by-product of international corporate greed.'

'Not cow in the accepted sense,' said Sir Branwell.

'Quite,' said Bognor. 'If the cow was not really a cow, but some sort of counterfeit cow in cow's clothing, then you'd expect the *Guardian* to be against it.'

'You two are being silly,' said Lady Fludd. 'This sort of conversation may be acceptable in the junior common room at Apocrypha, but it won't do here.'

The two Apocrypha men exchanged sheepish glances and acted as if chastened. Sometimes Bognor felt as if he had never really grown up. This sense was most acute when he

was with people he had known in the days of his youth. At
work, among those who, like him, passed themselves off as
adults and generally behaved in a fashion associated with
the grown-up, he too became mildly self-important and
serious. He didn't do jokes, or facetiousness of any kind.
He managed to become, frankly, a bit of a bore. This was
what seemed to be required among the seriously grown up.

'What about a cricket match?' said Monica, suddenly and
unexpectedly. 'You could have authors against publishers.'

'Writers don't play cricket,' said Bognor, swiftly, 'and
publishers don't play games outside the office. At least,
that's what I'm told.'

'Festivals,' said Sir Branwell, 'are about people droning
on. Some drone more effectively than others, but droning
is what everyone feels comfortable with. We don't want
innovation. Heaven forfend. Droning is what audiences
expect and what authors give them. We do one big drone.
Jolly effective and nobody has to do anything tiresome and
original.'

'Like think,' said his wife, crunching toast as if it were
yesterday's numbers.

'I always think,' said Lady Fludd, 'that cricket is a bit
like an author's drone. Interminable tedium during which
the audience sleeps or talks among themselves, punctu-
ated by sudden moments of unanticipated excitement
when the speaker's trousers fall down or he insults them
or something.'

'Not much unanticipated excitement in any authorial
drone I've ever slept through, eh, Simon,' said Sir Branwell,
'and as patron of my own lit fest, I've slept through a good
few in my time.'

'Quite,' said Bognor, not wishing, characteristically, to
give offence and sitting on the first one available. Fence,
that was. He had an uncomfortable habit of wordplay and
double entendre, which had got him into trouble when not
intended. Nevertheless, Bognor enjoyed weekends, especially in other people's houses. Weekends were good
anyway, because on the whole – with reservations and
disturbingly less as he grew older and the world round him

became more pointlessly frenetic – weekends were times when he was undisturbed by what was laughably described as 'work'. He had never really got the hang of this work thing which so captivated his successful contemporaries. His apparent insouciance regarding the occupation seemed to annoy them, but he couldn't really see the point of what other people described as work, and seemed on the whole to be a disagreeable activity whose only point seemed to be to generate sufficient funds to enjoy oneself when not working. During his lifetime, the amount of time most people needed to spend on 'work' in order to be able to enjoy their 'leisure' seemed to be increasing. He had read somewhere that this increase was 'exponential' and he had no doubt that it was. Indeed, he suspected that there was a rule lurking there. He had an uneasy feeling that one could learn the rule from teachers at business school. He, however, on the other hand, could not be bothered. Other people, more serious than he, were disparaging about this, but he just got on with life and savoured weekends such as this. Lazy occasions when all effort, however minimal, was expended by other people.

'Well,' said his wife, who was given to sudden bursts of energy which he generally discouraged, 'what exactly do we propose that we do today?'

'How do you mean "do"?' asked Sir Branwell, not looking up from his newspaper. He was also engaged with toast, so his words sounded furry and coated in crumb.

Sir Branwell, reflected Bognor, was one of him, and increasingly so. He was not much given to envy and wishing that he were other people, but in those rare moments when he played this game of make-believe, he found himself more and more wondering if it might be quite fun to be Sir Branwell. He drew the line at Lady Fludd however. Whereas Monica flirted dangerously with energy and enthusiasm, Lady Fludd appeared to subscribe to both with a passion. Bognor did not wish to be married to her. Life-swapping was one thing, and an idle hobby to be happily indulged. Wife-swapping, however, was something else altogether.

'Actually,' said Sir Branwell, looking around the table in

a breakfastly, blurry sort of a way, 'I don't think there is an awful lot to do, if you see what I mean. Everything is more or less taken care of. And, in a manner of speaking, and up to a point, er . . . done.'

He smiled affably and bit into his toast with more enthusiasm than he had spoken. If he had a consuming passion, which was not really his style, it was more for toast than for talk. This, reflected Bognor, was what life was about. A business efficiency expert, a visitor from Health and Safety or some similarly worthy quango, a government inspector, a jobsworth of whatever description, would have been appalled by this apparent inertia. Nothing was happening; nothing much seemed to matter. The females of the species displayed a slight sense of restlessnness, but this appeared to be easily quelled by their surroundings, if not by the somnolent, but presumably dominant, males. The males for their part resembled ancient lizards basking on warm stones in subtropical sunlight. They did not even spin. They did not even, like the lilies of the field, look good. They seemed completely devoid of purpose. There was no point to them.

Bognor sighed with profound satisfaction. Pointlessness was something to which, in his few introspective moments, he aspired. As he grew old he was getting better at it. He wondered if he should have another slice of toast, or a cup of tea; he was pleased by his indecision and reflecting on how an entire weekend could be spent contemplating such decisions, when the bell rang and his dream was destroyed.

They put up a fight against the intrusion.

'Rats!' said Sir Branwell, putting down his paper and his toast. 'I've told Brandon to fix that bloody bell.'

But Sir Branwell was wrong to blame it on the bell and it rang a second time, suggesting that the first ring was not haphazard and was caused, like the second, by a human agency. Someone had rung the front doorbell of the manor. On a Saturday morning. During breakfast. Unthinkable. But it had happened. It was a clear infringement of an unwritten rule. No one had rung the front doorbell on Saturday during breakfast during living memory. Yet it happened. Someone had.

The four looked at each other in shock and incredulity. One was not expecting the unexpected. One never was.

The bell rang a third time.

'Well cut along, darling,' said Lady Fludd. 'See who it is.'

Somewhere in the distance a dog barked. The staff, just the Brandons now, alas, always had most of the weekend off. Unless there was some sort of emergency. But when there *was* some sort of emergency, as now, they were never there. It was a rule of staff and there was nothing for it. Sir Branwell would have to open his front door himself.

He rose clumsily to his feet, grumbling in an incoherent rebarbative way, consistent with the occasion and with the disruption of well-established ritual.

Seconds later, he was back, energized, if such a thing were possible, and resembling the rural, aristocratic extramural equivalent of an action man. This was not particularly virile or particularly active, but it was a great deal more so than its virtually comatose predecessor.

In his wake, the baronet towed a woman, middle-aged, and middling in every visible sense except for her distress, which was extreme.

She seemed, for a moment, to be aware of the enormity of what she had done, but then, evidently, remembered why she was there and the reason for her distress.

'It's Sebastian,' she said. 'He's dead. Extremely. I mean he really is. Dead. He was all right when I last saw him but now he's dead. Gone. There was so much I wanted to say and so much I wanted to hear and now I can't, shan't. He's gone.'

Sir Branwell had produced brandy. His remedy for everything had been conjured up in a balloon on a silver salver that was originally presented to a great grandfather after some regimental triumph in the tug of war competition in Poona in the late nineteenth century. He always knew it would come in useful one-day. The present Sir Branwell that is, not the long-dead lieutenant with the electric whiskers and the faraway expression, who had been killed leading a charge against Boers in Africa.

'Drink this,' he said, as he had seen generations of stiff-lipped

English actors order in innumerable not very good movies. He thought of adding that it would do her good but decided he was muddling the movies up with the ads.

'Dorcas, how dreadful,' said Lady Fludd, laying down her paper and rising to her feet. 'You poor sausage. How dreadful.'

She was thinking at the same time as she spoke, rather than planning ahead. This was a mistake. Her words did not convey what she really meant. She didn't really think the event dreadful; nor had she really meant to call Dorcas a sausage. It just came out like that.

Privately, she was thinking as she spoke, but the poor sausage was herself and even though she was commenting privately on the dreadfulness of the event, what she was actually saying was, 'Bloody vicar. How incredibly inconvenient. And just before the festival. But then Sebastian always was a selfish little sod.'

Out loud, however, she said, consolingly again, 'You poor sausage! Sit down, sit down for heaven's sake.'

THREE

Brigadier Horace was a barking brigadier but he had little or no bite.

'All fang but no finish!' said Sir Branwell, with whom he had been at school, or thought he might have been. He was too polite to ask. Or indolent. Or, more likely, uninterested. He neither knew nor cared with whom he had been at school. In any event, people were at school with him, not him with them. The difference was crucial. 'Never seen a shot fired in anger, let alone pulled a trigger.'

Contractor had done the work. He had done so at his master's behest, his master being in the wrong place and, in a manner of speaking, on holiday. He had done so with flair, invention and assiduity. Contractor didn't do competence. He obviously deployed sources, but he did not attribute his work in a conventional academic way, with footnotes and bibliography at the bottom of the page or the end of the book. Instead, he did so like a card sharp. Now you see me, now you don't. He flickered magically with a sense of legerdemain, like a conjuror facing befuddled males on a drunken stag night. Here a rabbit, there a beauty in a bathing suit sawn in half, here a glass of water disappearing, only to re-emerge behind an ear or in a far corner of a room. Always the top hat, always the cane, always the fixed grin, but never anything conventional.

This was why Bognor had hired him. His first in semiotics from the University of Wessex was neither here nor there. Nor was his race, parentage or sexual orientation. Bognor liked him because he was bright and quirky. Other people found this intimidating. In the unlikely event that they appreciated intellect and industry and the qualifications which were the inevitable result, they liked them orthodox. In a super competent world, those who believed that two plus two always equalled four were appreciated; only a genius or a poltroon would think they added up to anything else. Contractor wasn't sure they did and he certainly was not a poltroon. Bognor liked this; and Contractor knew that he liked it, and as he grew older he realized that this appreciation of his intellectual eccentricity was unusual. It was one of the things that made Bognor different. It infuriated some, particularly if they were bright and successful. A minority, however, found the quality appealing. One of these was Harvey Contractor and he was very, very bright. Formidably so.

Take Brigadier Blenkinsop. Eustace Basil Blenkinsop, aka 'Basher' Blenkinsop. Educated Wellington and RMA Sandhurst. The brigadier came from a long line of retired majors, though his father was a vicar in the Quantocks. Stogumber. St Mary's. Red sandstone. The church was famous for its candlelit chandelier discovered by one of the brigadier's father's predecessors in 1907, languishing. It was now lit on high days and holy days and looked very beautiful.

Bognor shut his eyes and thought of the candles in the chandelier at Christmas in St Mary's Stogumber. He imagined the vicar clambering up into the pulpit and saying words that none of his congregation understood. Stogumber wasn't exactly the centre of the universe even when Basher was growing up. There was a sister who was married to a vet on Vancouver Island and another sister who was a spinster in Letchworth and did good works. That was all. Bognor imagined what it must have been like growing up as the only son of a vicar in rural Somerset. Was the vicar embittered? A fire and brimstone man? A pacifist? Had his religion influenced the brigadier?

After Sandhurst, Blenkinsop had gone into the gunners. Blenkinsop's outfit was the 13th Mobile. Its proper name was the '13th Mobile Artillery', because since Agincourt, and possibly earlier, they had been able to deploy lethal weaponry in the least expected places. There were no earlier twelve mobile artillery units, thus earning the 13th the unusual sobriquet of 'the Lucky for some' though they were usually known simply as the '13th Mobile'. Another nickname was the 'Cautious Cauliflowers', which derived from their habit of pinning a floret of the vegetable next to their cap badges every Dettingen Day. This was the anniversary of the battle of 1743, which was the last occasion on which an English – actually German – monarch had led his men into battle. This only happened because the CO of the 13th, Colonel 'Biffer' Lowe-Laugher, had stuck a prong of his tuning fork into the reluctant rump of the king's horse. Hence the regimental custom of placing a gilt tuning fork on the Colonel's right every night at the Dettingen dinner. The British army was full of such things.

At school and the academy, Blenkinsop had boxed and he went on fighting with some success after joining the army. He was battalion welterweight champion and knocked out some sergeant who was much fancied in the ring. As Second Lieutenant Blenkinsop he competed in the army championship, but was defeated by a mad captain in the Irish Guards. Bognor wondered what the Vicar of Stogumber made of his son's pugilism.

The vicar of Stogumber had briefly taught at a public school – of which Bognor had not previously heard – in Warminster. He guessed it must have closed. The Queen's School. Queen's Warminster. Contractor had drawn a blank here because the school was long closed and all records lost or destroyed. Nevertheless, it seemed that the Reverend Blenkinsop had spent a relatively short time at the school before being translated to Stogumber. Again, there was no record. Why had Blenkinsop senior spent so short a time at Queen's Warminster? Why had he been translated so swiftly to such a relative backwater? Bognor was suspicious. His wife, Muriel, was the daughter of a general, a friend and protégé of Field Marshal Haig in World War One. That too aroused Bognor's suspicion, though he was not sure precisely why. Muriel had a posthumous reputation in West Somerset for prodigious snobbery, whereas her husband was known throughout the area as a man of the people.

What was undoubtedly suspicious was the presence in the regiment of a young chaplain named Fludd.

Forget brigadiers, thought Bognor. Life was full of people

who had risen to the surface of life like scum on stock, and Brigadier Horace was one such. Bognor regarded himself as a front-line soldier – the sort of man who, at the Battle of the Somme in the Great War, would have gone over the top in front of his platoon, been cut to pieces by enemy machine gun fire and won a posthumous Military Cross. Horace Blenkinsop, the barking brigadier, would meanwhile have been watching events, if at all, through binoculars in a requisitioned chateau, while stuffing his face with stolen champagne and plover's eggs.

Bognor recalled his grandfather, a veteran of this very campaign, gassed and now gone to God, telling him that in his battalion, as in others, they had something called HQ company. No one knew what men in HQ company actually did, except issue more and more pieces of regulatory paper with which the rest of the battalion wiped their bottoms. During the war, more and more people gravitated to HQ company, where they performed more and more meaningless rituals, whose only apparent purpose was to make life diffi-cult to impossible for those who actually did the work. Life, said Bognor's grandfather, was much the same: far too many people in HQ company getting in the way of men on the ground trying to do a decent day's work, like him and his grandson.

Thus Brigadier Blenkinsop. Yet, such was life that Brigadier Blenkinsop was widely regarded as a bit of a catch. He made programmes for television about battles in which he had not fought and of which he knew little. He opined in the *Daily Telegraph* and other public prints, telling his fellow man what to think about military warfare, but also everything else from greenhouse emissions (a fiction, fanned by leftist scaremongers) to railway trains (vanished due to that damned fellow Beeching) and gastronomy (days were when a celebrity chef was just a cook and garlic was something Johnny Foreigner used to flavour horse-meat).

Bognor did not care for the brigadier or for his sort. Whitehall was rife with brigadiers, barking orders, strutting about and getting in the way. Nevertheless, and notwith-standing, you had to hand it to him. Bognor was reminded of an elderly English rugby footballer, a cumbersome number eight, who, way past his prime, somehow survived, and indeed prospered, where younger, fitter, more agile and talented rivals came and usually went. This was achieved by stealth and what a dead journalist, much admired by Bognor, once described as 'rat-like cunning'. This was possessed in spades by the ancient rumbling English rugby player. He read the game with deceptive ease and was able to anticipate its direction with unerring precision. So, without apparent effort or indeed movement, or endeavour of all but the most notional kind, he was always able to be at the centre of important play, where his strength and experience proved decisive. Others ran hither and yon, charging about like headless chickens, while the old bull elephant surged magnificently, and in an almost stately manner, through the wildest passages of the game.

So it was with the brigadier. Throughout his life, he seemed, uncannily, always to be in the right place at the right time. When dead men's shoes needed to be filled, the brigadier was always close by, available to step into them at a moment's notice. When a desk needed to be driven or an opinion expressed, Horace was available, amenable, willing and able. By his expert reading of the game of life, he had always been able to keep at least a pace or two ahead of his often more talented rivals, without exposing himself to needless risk, hazard or what they might have described as effort of any kind. His was a triumph of cunning over exertion, of wise inertia as compared with the charge of the light brigade. His was a staff officer's life, the epitome of one who had spent his time in the cushioned security of HQ company. And it was he who was to be the keynote speaker at this year's festival, and getting him was considered rather a coup.

Horace and his wife, Esther, had spent the previous night at what had, for many years, been called the Fludd Arms, but had recently been rechristened the Two by Two, after it had been sold off by Sir Branwell to a young man from the East End of London, who had reinvented himself as Gunther Battenburg and turned the ancient hostelry into a

gastropub, to the consternation of the local community and
to the interested attention of inspectors from the *Michelin
Guide* and others. It had also begun to attract a significant
and, to Sir Branwell and Lady Fludd, unwelcome sort of
visitor. They took photographs of each other during meal
times and came for the slug muesli, the squirrel pavlova
and the *oeufs ananas*. They had more money than sense,
lived off bonuses and were, in a word, trendy. Sir Branwell
regarded them much as he did seagulls and would have
treated them similarly, given half a chance. He longed to
have them up before him when he, or Camilla, were sitting
on the bench, but so far neither he nor his wife had had the
pleasure.

If the Reverend Sebastian had indeed been done in by an
alien hand, then Brigadier Horace, the brigadier's wife,
Esther, and Gunther Battenburg would have to join the long
list of suspects. Battenburg was gay and had no known
partner. That is to say, he had formed no regular attachment
and was for the purposes of the impending enquiry, single.
This 'long list', including most residents of Mallborne,
would, presumably, be narrowed down before too long,
rather in the manner of literary prizes such as the Booker,
the Costa and, indeed, the newly inaugurated Flanagan Fludd
for the best novel with a beginning, a middle and an end.
Of this, Sir Branwell had high hopes. He very much hoped
that this unfortunate incident would not cause them to be
dashed, or even put on ice for the time being.

'Poor timing,' said Sir Branwell, later in the library. 'But
then timing was never one of Sebastian's things. Not that
Sebastian did "things" when you come to think about it.
"Things" weren't Sebastian's kind of thing, if you see what
I mean.'

'No,' agreed Bognor, who understood perfectly. He was
sometimes accused of not understanding even quite obvious
matters. In fact, he understood more than others suspected
and quite often more than was good for him. 'Not a popular
man, Sebastian.'

'No,' Sir Branwell said, 'not unduly.'

'So, no real friends but no real enemies either?'

'You could say that.' His host frowned.

'Have you noticed,' said Bognor, 'that popularity nowadays breeds popularity? It's the reverse of what I think we were taught at Apocrypha.'

'That the eclectic and unusual was preferable to received wisdom.'

'Something like that,' said Bognor. 'Nowadays we are all more or less victims of herd instinct. If everybody likes something it is automatically good. A best-seller is better than something only a minority admires. Majority taste is good taste.'

'That's new?'

'I think so, yes. In the old days someone like the Reverend Sebastian would have been accepted in a way that he wasn't nowadays.'

'Because he was odd?'

'Maybe,' said Bognor, 'maybe not.' He was thinking. It made him frown. 'It's to do with dumbing down. We distrust anything that's out of the ordinary. We live in the age of the common man. If the common man thinks something's good, then it is by definition good. If not, it's unpopular. Ergo bad.'

'Elitist?' asked Sir Branwell who recognized the argument and sympathized with it.

'Could be,' said Bognor, 'but not necessarily so. Manchester United are popular and excellent. Accrington Stanley less so. That doesn't make Accrington Stanley bad.'

'But they *are* bad. Man U would have them for breakfast any day of the week.'

They were getting into irrelevant waters, the land of the red herring. Bognor tried bringing them back to something approaching Earth.

'Are we saying that the vicar was murdered because he was no good? A sort of ecclesiastical equivalent of a team that lurches between the lower divisions of the football league and something sponsored by a cement company.'

'No,' said Bognor, thoughtfully. 'The Reverend Sebastian sounds like a man with few friends, but, by the same token, he probably had few enemies. He was too Laodicean to aspire to either. Difficult to be enthusiastic about someone lukewarm.'

'I wouldn't describe Sebastian as "lukewarm",' said Sir Branwell. 'Useless, yes; lukewarm, no. He had some strong opinions. Women priests, Muslim fundamentalists. Strong, very.'

'Pro or anti?'

'Pro. Sebastian was teetering on the brink of being radical. Never over the edge, being one of life's teeterers. He was always on, or near a brink, but never quite over.'

Bognor smiled. 'You didn't like him.'

His old chum smiled back. 'I don't think liking really came into it. That was the point about Sebby. You didn't like him or dislike him. He just was, if you see what I mean.'

'High church?'

'High on the whole,' said Sir Branwell. 'Keen on smells and bells. Latin. But a soft spot for that American-Kiwi monk, Merton, which puts him on the left, I would think. Difficult to pigeonhole Sebastian, which was one of his few attractive features. You never knew what he was going to think about anything. Come to think of it, I don't suppose he had much of a clue himself.'

'Bit of a ditherer as well as a teeterer,' said Bognor.

'Uncertainty was his middle name,' said the squire. 'Except when he was certain of something. That's one thing you can say for him. Well, could say for him, when he was, well, you know, alive. He was assailed by doubt. I rather approve of doubt.'

'Up to a point,' said Bognor, repeating an Apocrypha adage. They both recognized it and grinned.

'So, in an age of certainty he was a prey to doubt,' said Bognor, 'and in an age when popularity was a mark of merit, he was prepared to be unpopular. Sounds rather a good thing.'

'No, not at all,' said Sir Branwell. 'That's far too positive. He was never that black and white.'

'No,' said Bognor. He could see that the vicar had been a tiresome priest, if seldom turbulent. Turbulence was obviously not in his nature, which was a pity as far as Sir Simon was concerned, as he had a definite weak spot for turbulence of almost every description. Perhaps the vicar had, as it were, kicked his own bucket; taken his own life; died by his own. Yet suicide, despite a popular view that it constituted cowardice – not a view to which Bognor ever ascribed – required a certainty, not to mention a moral courage, which was not part of the former padre's make-up. Bognor was not at all sure what had happened in the night, but he was pretty sure it wasn't suicide. Something had clearly gone bump but the drama had been inflicted by an outside agency. Of that he was already certain. He felt it in his water, which was, on the whole, and on the evidence of past history, as good an indicator as any.

He said so out loud, seeking confirmation, and was glad to receive it.

'I don't think he killed himself,' he said. 'It doesn't sound in character.'

Sir Branwell shook his head sadly. 'I think you're right,' he said. 'For all kinds of reason. Nevertheless, I find it hard to believe that anyone would have done such a thing on purpose. It seems to me much more like a hideous mistake.' Sir Branwell was a cock-up man rather than a conspiracy theorist. He held to the belief that when 'Crusoe', the great Somerset fast bowler and scribe killed himself, he overdosed by mistake. Chaps made mistakes. Name of the game. Fact of life. Could be awkward, but most real awkwardness was the product of confusion and inertia, not malice aforethought.

'Hideous mistake, eh?'

Bognor laughed mirthlessly, having been taught, like his host, that clichés were full of dangerous assumptions and prejudices.

'For once,' he said, 'the mistake really would have been hideous. Not often you can say that, eh?'

FOUR

The chief constable was, as usual, brisk and efficient. Actually this was not true. The chief constable was the reason the boys were in the library, and it was into the library that the chief constable was ushered by Brandon the butler. Brandon did for the Fludds upstairs, while Mrs Brandon toiled away below stairs, behind the baize and below the salt. She was the invisible half, while her husband was all mouth and striped trouser. He buttled; she cooked; he was the outward sign that all was well; she the inner strength that ensured it really, almost, was. Time was when the manor would have supported a staff of several, if not of thousands. Now it was just the two of them: Harry and Peggoty.

'Black, two sugars,' said the chief constable. He shot with Sir Branwell; his wife played bridge with Sir Branwell's wife. They were both 'county'.

The chief constable, whose name was Jones, came from elsewhere but was 'county' by rank and assimilation. He was also living proof of the fact that in modern Britain, still, there were two sides to almost every question: the visible and the invisible. With the post-Murdoch decline in the concept of the Fourth Estate and of the press as a tribune of the people, the invisible side of British life had become more significant and the visible more perfunctory. Nevertheless, the distinction was maintained. There was a way in which things were seen to be done and there was a way in which things were actually done. This distinction was further complicated by the twin and, on the whole, contrary distinctions between 'conspiracy' and 'cock-up'.

It was widely believed that these two theories stood for an 'either or'; that you either had a conspiracy or you had a cock-up, and that this explained everything. However, Bognor's life experience, contrary to that of Sir Branwell

and others, suggested that the two ideas were not altern-
atives and that the British had an unusual, possibly unique,
propensity for combining the two. This meant that life was
either a conspiratorial cock-up or a cocked-up conspiracy
– probably both. The British had an almost unerring gift
for getting things hopelessly wrong. They also possessed
an apparently limitless capacity for gossip and plotting, as
in Gunpowder and Popish. The Gunpowder Plot was a
brilliant example of a conspiratorial cock-up and a cocked-
up conspiracy. As far as Bognor was concerned, Guy, or
Guido Fawkes, was the ultimate Englishman. He wondered
if he was an ancestor of Sebastian, the writer, but it was an
idle and irrelevant wonder and not one worth worrying
about. The Fawkes of gunpowder, treason and plot – the
man for whom one still paid a penny before setting fire to
him every November 5th – may not have been the greatest
Englishman ever, but he was the most English.

Chief Constable Jones had arrived to explain the invisible
solution to the questions posed by the death of the Reverend
Sebastian Fludd. It was obviously suicide. He had assigned
one of his most trusted lieutenants, a detective chief
inspector, no less, to the case and this man was adept at
going through the necessary motions with absolute convic-
tion. He would examine the scene of crime and the body
– or rather he would cause minions to do so, for even in
make-believe DCIs did not get their hands dirty – and then
he would report. He would issue dozens of reports, all
beautifully typed. This would be done by other minions, for
chief constables did not type. In this case, typing was a skill
that the chief constable had not seen fit to acquire. He was
a good shot though; a skill that he had acquired relatively
late in life, through the offices of his ambitious wife who
recognized that shooting was still, in the county, a skill
essential for social advancement.

Sir Branwell had shot since he was so high. Bognor did
not shoot, never having seen the point. He ate birds mowed
down by others but deplored their turning it into sport. His
disapproval was, however, mild and did not extend to the
table.

Chief Constable Jones said the suicide was sad, that the balance of the poor man's mind had obviously been disturbed, but that he would have wished life, and more particularly, the festival, to go on as near to normal as was decently possible. The chief constable had not yet won his knighthood. Bognor had, risibly, acquired his; Sir Branwell's came as his natural inheritance.

'I'm not at all sure he did kill himself,' said Sir Simon.

'Sir Simon thinks it was murder,' said Sir Branwell. He laid emphasis on the word 'sir' and noticed that the chief constable noticed. This pleased him.

Mr Jones shrugged a man-of-the-world shrug and smiled what was meant to be a man-of-the-world smile but came out as more of a pained rictus.

'Maybe it was and maybe it wasn't,' he said, 'but it will be much more convenient all round if it's suicide. And seen to be so. I'm sure that can be arranged. The local press is very good. Editor has a decent handicap. We play eighteen holes every Thursday at Royal Mallborne. Suicide's the ticket. Much the best for everyone.'

'Not for the widow,' said Bognor. 'If it's suicide, the insurance company won't pay up.'

'Oh,' said the chief constable, 'God will provide.'

'Doubt it,' said Sir Branwell. 'His people are strapped for cash right now. The diocese made some ill-advised investments in Iceland. Besides, the Lord thy God is inclined to be a bit tight where lucre is concerned. His son came down to tell us it was filthy and diminished one's chances of making it upstairs. Eyes of needles, camels, haystacks and all that.' He paused, proud of his Biblical knowledge. Bognor was impressed; the policeman less so.

'My professional opinion is that it was suicide,' said the man Jones.

Neither Sir Branwell nor Bognor gave a fig for his professional opinion.

'Sir Simon's professional opinion is that it could perfectly well have been murder.'

The chief constable was on the brink of saying that he didn't give much of a fig for Bognor's professional opinion but evidently thought better of it, and before he made a fool of himself simply repeated two words.

'Professional opinion?' he said, inviting explanation.

'I'm sorry,' said Sir Branwell, not sorry at all, 'I should have said that Sir Simon runs SIDBOT – The Special Investigations Department of the Board of Trade. There's very little in the field of crime that he hasn't solved in his day. The murder of Champion Whately Wonderful, Britain's Prize Poodle; skulduggery in one of our best known monastic communities; Fleet Street; the Stately Home Industry; Canada; publishing; even the sudden and unexpected death of the Master of our own dear college. You name it and Sir Simon has been there. And he always gets his man.'

'Well,' Bognor had the decency to look mildly, if not wholly, embarrassed, pinkening a shade and shuffling his feet in a less than convincing suggestion that his host had been over-egging the pudding, 'I wouldn't put it quite like that.'

Chief Constable Jones was visibly shaken. He had taken Bognor for one of life's failures, like so many of Sir Branwell's friends. He seemed so understated, so frayed at the edges, so positively unremarkable. In the normal course of events the chief constable would probably not have noticed him. In this the chief constable would have been wrong as usual, but his would have been a common enough reaction. Bognor was not instantly noticeable and this was part of the reason for his success. He grew on one like ivy on a wall or moss on an unturned stone. Men like Jones often failed to notice and when they finally did, it was too late.

'You don't think it was suicide, Sir Simon.' The chief constable was careful to remember the knighthood, to which he and, more keenly Mrs Jones, aspired.

'Neither of us are attracted to the idea,' said Bognor. 'It seems too obvious. And not in character. Or not, at least, from what I know of the man. There was no note.'

'No note.'

'No note.'

Silence enwrapped them.

'In my experience of suicide, which I may say is considerable, there is usually a note,' said Jones. 'Just because a note has not yet been found does not necessarily mean that there is no note. Or indeed notes. Sometimes the deceased sends several.'

'The Reverend Sebastian was not,' said the patron of his living, 'a man of many words. Except when he took to the pulpit.'

'Shy or just . . . er, laconic . . . ?' asked Bognor.

'Economic with words,' said his namesake. 'Believed that actions spoke louder. Tended to leave matters unminced except at matins.'

'In any event,' said Jones, sounding like the man of the world he wanted to be, 'suicide would, generally speaking, be a much more convenient verdict.'

The other two looked at him incredulously. Both, in their different ways, led sheltered lives. Here was the force of law and order expressing a preference for convenience over truth. Both Bognor and Fludd had a naive belief that the police believed in justice and the triumph of good over evil. Yet, here was a top police person suggesting, as far as they could see, that a man had not been murdered because the investigation and the concomitant apparatus would be too much bother.

'But what if he were killed?' asked Sir Branwell, as mildly as he could manage while still being polite.

'So what?' asked Mr Jones, meaning to sound rhetorical and wringing his hands. 'A murder enquiry involves an inordinate amount of fuss. There will be officers, uniformed and uninformed all over the place. The press, possibly even national, will descend like vultures. There will be television cameras; statements to be taken; lines to be drawn. The whole thing will be excessively tedious.'

'That's the way with British justice,' said Bognor. Had Jones known him better, he would have noticed that there was an edge to Bognor's voice at this point and that this edge suggested danger. He should have been alerted and gone into back-pedalling mode. Instead, he blundered on.

'We're here to ensure a quiet, orderly life,' he told them,

in words that he had obviously uttered before. Often. 'The job of the police is the same as that of all authority, namely to maintain an orderly society, prevent undue irregularity, alarms, excursions and things that bring other things into disrepute. There are necessarily times when in order to maintain a sense of order and common sense, corners have to be cut and a certain economy with regard to the truth has to be effected. That is why we employ public relations officers and other consultants. We seek to allay fears and to facilitate the order of the day. So, suicide, which is regrettable but rocks no boats, is preferable to murder, which upsets people.'

'So, the police hoodwinks the public and turns a blind eye when it suits them,' said Bognor with deceptive blandness.

'In a manner of speaking,' said the chief constable, 'though I'd be unlikely to say so in public.' He laughed mirthlessly. 'My PR people wouldn't allow it.'

Neither Bognor nor Sir Branwell joined in.

'I was always taught,' said Sir Branwell, 'that justice not only had to be done, but had to be seen to be done.'

The chief constable, believing that he had won the day, was well into his stride, 'That's a very old-fashioned way of looking at things,' he said. 'Seeing is now believing. The vital thing is that justice must be seen to be done. Whether or not it really has is neither here nor there. Life is a game of smoke and mirrors. Providing these are convincing, nothing else matters.'

He smiled, evidently pleased with himself. He had only expressed the truth as he and his colleagues saw it. This nonsense about reality was as old-fashioned as the belief in truth and justice which one or two of his colleagues still banged on about. What actually happened was of no concern to the man in the street. The man in the street was fed a pabulum, a placebo, a lie if you insisted, which kept up his morale and him or her out of mischief. If the reality was different, what the hell. The fewer people knew the facts of life, the better for all concerned.

He was surprised therefore to discover that Sir Branwell

was thanking him for his time and concern, and telling him that Brandon the butler would show him out.

He usually reckoned on a glass of sherry when visiting a Lord Lieutenant.

Bognor was sorry that he hadn't asked Harvey Contractor to run a finger around the inside of the chief constable's collar, but he hadn't. Nor Mrs Jones, who sounded even worse. But chief constables didn't do murders. Likewise the butler and Mrs Brandon. The butler never dunnit. Nor his wife. Even so . . .

FIVE

The departure of the chief constable created less of a vacuum than he would have wished.

'Phew!' said Bognor.

'What a ghastly little oik!' said Sir Branwell.

'You mustn't say things like that,' said Bognor. 'It's incredibly old-fashioned, snobbish and politically incorrect.'

'True though.' Sir Branwell smiled roguishly.

Bognor did not agree, nor disagree, merely looked pained.

Growing up, the word 'oik' had been a sort of universal pejorative such as 'pseudo', which stood for 'pseudo-intellectual', meaning, in a particularly philistine society, anyone who had read, much less enjoyed, a book. 'Grey' as in 'grey man' was another all-purpose term of abuse, which signified nothing more than a general dislike. Over the years, however, 'oik' had acquired social undertones which Bognor did not remember. 'Oik' was how posh people referred to those they regarded as their social inferiors. That, at least, had become the universal perception which meant that the word had slipped out of the lexicon. People like Sir Branwell still used it, however, at least in private. People like Sir Branwell assumed that Bognor did the same. This was not true and at times he resented it. At others it suited him.

'I don't think your vicar killed himself,' he said.

'I agree,' said Branwell.

'But your man Jones is keen to disagree because it's tidier and more convenient. I don't think we should let him.'

'Seconded,' said Branwell.

They paused to congratulate themselves on their commitment to fair play. This was an old-fashioned concept but one in which they both had some belief, along with decency and common sense. Greed and convenience had, on the whole and up to a point, taken their place and they both disliked these characteristics with a passion. In Sir Branwell's case, this had a lot to do with finding them vulgar, common and, in a word 'oikish'. His was a liberalism founded on class; Bognor's on an innate sense of what was proper. At times these collided but they were not quite, nor always, the same. Bognor liked a lot of the noise but that didn't mean that he believed it. Second-hand car salesmen came with braying accents and a lack of chin. Officers did not enjoy a monopoly of proper values. Far from it. Bognor was, in some respects, one of life's corporals; Sir Branwell would have been a second-lieutenant on the Somme and driven a railway engine during the General Strike. He was in favour of corporal punishment and against the duvet.

In any case, his beliefs were far from strident. He did not like to shout or seem shrill. Nods, winks, handshakes and words unsaid were his way of doing things.

'Trouble is,' he said, 'that his writ runs.'

'Meaning?'

Bognor told him that the chief constable controlled the local police force and they were the authority charged with the investigation of suspicious death.

'But I'm the Lord Lieutenant.' And he told Bognor of a recurring dream in which the Dowager Duchess of some-where or other caused wooden legs, containing game pie at one end and fudge at the other, to be dropped from a light aircraft for the benefit of those who worked on the estate. Sir Branwell thought this might be significant. Bognor, sceptical about dreams at the best of times and even when their symbolism was obvious, forbore to comment.

'Any chance of a coffee?' he asked instead.

By way of answer, Sir Branwell searched for a bell-push under the carpet and pressed it with one toe of an uncharacteristically monogrammed slipper from Dunhill. The slipper had been some sort of offer. Presently, Brandon came buttling in and was sent for coffee.

Bognor was very unclear about the position of Lord Lieutenant; only vaguely aware that it meant less than it once had. Also that the role of the chief constable was becoming more important in similar proportion. Thus, the one had diminished, was diminishing and seemed likely to be diminished still further, while the other was comparably enhanced.

'Does a chief constable outrank a Lord Lieutenant?' he asked ingenuously.

'Certainly not,' replied Sir Branwell. 'At least not yet, and most definitely not in this neck of the woods. As long as I'm around, I'm in charge. On behalf of Her Gracious Majesty, God bless her.'

Bognor wasn't so sure of this, much as he admired his old friend's confidence.

'We'll have to be clever.'

'Naturally.' Sir Branwell never allowed his 4th class honours degree to interfere with his assurance on this account.

Bognor couldn't help feeling that things had come to a pretty pass when a Lord Lieutenant and the Board of Trade's head of special investigations had to resort to subterfuge in order to ensure rights that were supposed to have been established almost eight hundred years earlier. But then things had come to a pretty pass. He was aware of that.

'Assuming our man was murdered, who would have done it? And who could have done it?'

The squire thought for a moment. 'Opportunity is almost universal,' he said, after a moment's reflection. 'Motive practically the reverse.'

'Yes,' said Bognor, wanting and needing more.

'Well,' said Sir Branwell, 'the padre was in the habit of going to his church for a bit of solitary rehearsal, communion with his Lord and whatever took his fancy before preaching the following day. He was very much a creature of habit. Everyone knew that he was due to preach the opening festival sermon – which, incidentally, we had better cancel – and that therefore he would be alone in church the evening before. Solitary and vulnerable.'

'No need to cancel,' said Bognor unexpectedly and at an apparent tangent. 'I'll preach.'

'You what?' Sir Branwell had not been expecting this.

'I said I'll preach,' said Bognor. 'Could be a useful

opportunity to pre-empt some thunderous chief constabular strike.'

'But you've never preached before in your life.'

'Always a first time,' said Bognor, with a characteristic lack of modesty. 'And I've always fancied it. Nice frock, captive audience, pulpit. Ask Monica. Being a bishop was always one of my several ambitions. I'd have made rather a good bishop. Pope, even.'

'He captains one of the other teams,' said Sir Branwell, who had taken to the pulpit on a number of occasions in his role as one of the county's great and good. He too rather rated himself on the sermon front, though with better evidence than his contemporary. He had to concede, however, that Bognor had the better degree.

'I'd have been a perfectly acceptable Mullah and a decent enough rabbi,' said Bognor, not wholly facetiously. 'I might not have been quite so hot on the Indian fakir front. Swami Simon doesn't tremendously appeal, though I quite fancy the frock and the beard.'

'Not to mention the sex.'

'Much exaggerated, I'm told,' he said. 'Besides, I have a feeling Monica might have views on the matter, and if it came to a head-to-head between the Lord God Almighty and my wife, I know who I'm backing.'

'So,' said Sir Branwell, returning to his subject in a single leap, 'when it comes to opportunity, the world is your oyster. When we're dealing with motive, the oyster becomes shut like a trap. There aren't any. Traps, that is. Nor much in the way of motive. As for opportunities . . .' He seemed suddenly thoughtful.

'Well,' said Bognor, being constructive, *'cherchez la femme*. In the absence of any other suspects that's where one is always taught to start. *La femme*. Crime *passionelle*.'

'I hardly think . . .' began Sir Branwell. 'But then . . . well . . . poor sausage.' He recalled the messenger who had, as it were, brought the bad news from Ghent. 'You mean Dorcas. *Cherchez* Dorcas. It doesn't sound convincing. I'm not convinced. I doubt you'll convince a jury. Or a judge. Not by starting with Dorcas.'

'We have to begin with someone,' said Bognor. 'And if Dorcas is the only candidate, then we have to begin with Dorcas. Is there . . . was there anyone else?'

'Of course not.' Sir Branwell seemed incensed. 'Sebastian was the most chaste man I ever knew. I assume he and Dorcas must once have enjoyed some sort of carnal relations. Otherwise they wouldn't have had the two children. But if virgin birth was a human possibility, you'd have to put up Sebastian and Dorcas as prime candidates for virgin parenthood. Whatever else it may have been, you can't imagine sex with those two being anything other than a sacred duty. A bit of a chore. Certainly not fun.'

He paused, possibly imagining sex in the other Fludd household, and briefly shuddered. He was basically rather keen on sex; the Sebastian-Fludds weren't. End of story. The Sebastian-Fludds weren't built for it either. Different chapter, same book. Shame that *droit de seigneur* had gone out with the ark. He was rather in favour, but there were certain things best left unsaid.

'So, the Reverend Sebastian wasn't the victim of a crime *passionelle*? At least not in a conventional sense.' Bognor seemed thoughtful. He had seen enough of life, and more particularly of death, to rule out crimes of passion even in unlikely candidates. Perhaps, most of all, in unlikely candidates. Still waters could run exceedingly deep. Springs sprung in unexpected places. He was disinclined to rule out something to do with sex where the vicar was concerned.

'How many festival performers were in town already?' he asked, changing tack unexpectedly, though sex and the festival performer could not be ruled out at this stage either.

Sir Branwell thought.

'Not many, as far as I know,' he said. 'The Brigadier and Mrs Brigadier. Vicenza Book.'

'Not *the* Vicenza Book?'

'Why? Do you know her?'

'She's famous,' said Bognor, irritably. 'Even I have heard of Vicenza Book. She's probably the most famous soprano in world opera.'

'I wouldn't know,' said Sir Branwell, who didn't.

'Monica will be incredibly overexcited,' said Bognor. '*The Nightingale of Padella* in Brodo. Italy's Stoke on Trent. We heard her do an obscure Handel with the ENO.'

'Yes. Well,' said Branwell, 'her father used to work behind the bar in the pub when it was still a recognizable pub. Her mother's Italian. Hence Padella in whatsit. She was, as it were, passing. She and Bert didn't last long and she took the girl back to Italy. Bert died. Drank himself to death. Sad story. Vicenza wrote out of the blue saying she'd like to come and sing at the festival, had such happy memories of Mallborne, blah, blah. Sebastian was all for it. All for her. So we signed her up. She should be here. She's taken a house with her camp followers.'

'And she's already in town?'

'Stretch limo sighted shortly before lunch yesterday. Not many of those in Mallborne. Tinted glass. White. Personalized number plate.'

'Sounds authentic,' Bognor conceded.

'Anyone else?'

'Martin Allgood.'

'The novelist?' Bognor had read an Allgood once and didn't like it.

'He's this year's writer-in-residence. Here for the duration. Does lots of readings, interviews, judging of things. We put him in Thatch Cottage on the estate and call it the Writer's House for the week. Rather a good publicity stunt. Always attracts masses of publicity, and Allgood can be relied on to say something suitably foul and controversial. We had him once before, about ten years ago. Seemed surprisingly nice actually. Pretty girlfriend but I think she's done a bunk. I read an interview with him a year or so ago which seemed to suggest he batted and bowled. AC/DC.'

'Probably another publicity stunt.' Bognor had a low opinion of Allgood based mainly on the one reading of the single book – something to do with expectations. Not great in Allgood's case. He knew this to be unfair, but was convinced that the author was an untalented showman. He had a beard and was very short. Bognor had an aversion to small, hairy writers, which was based entirely on prejudice but was more or less unshakeable, probably for that very reason.

'Was Sebastian the vicar during Allgood's previous residency?' asked Bognor, quick as the proverbial flash. He liked not to be seen missing tricks, especially when so clumsily flaunted.

'As a matter of fact, Sebastian was newly arrived. They didn't get on. Allgood criticized Sebby's sermon, which was ill-advised. He was sensitive about his sermons, Sebastian.'

'Don't blame him,' said Bognor. 'What was the point of Allgood's criticism?'

'Oh, Allgood was going through a Dawkins' atheist phase as usual and Sebastian was sympathetic to the creationist johnnies. Not hook-line-and-sinkered, but sympathetic. Sebastian had a fatal tendency to see all sides to an argument; Allgood only ever saw one.'

'Seldom the same,' smiled Bognor.

'No one ever accused Martin of consistency,' said Sir Branwell. 'Not even Martin, and a lot of the time he is his own worst enemy. As he freely admits.'

'Did he dislike the vicar enough to kill him?'

The squire thought for a moment. 'At the time, maybe. But Allgood never harboured anything for very long. Least of all grudges. And these days he's something of a creationist himself. If you believe what you read in the papers.'

'No.' Bognor grinned. 'I don't.'

He didn't either.

Bognor reflected that he had included his old friends in Contractor's brief. The office genius had duly obliged. But.

Neither Branwell nor Camilla had escaped Contractor's forensic attentions. They couldn't. What's more, they would both have been mortified if they had been left out. There was nothing in the reports of his two old friends that caused Bognor to so much as raise an eyebrow. Nevertheless, he felt as if he we were reading an obituary by a professional who hadn't known the deceased, or a eulogy by a friend of a friend at one of those impersonal memorial services. Too often, the preacher hadn't known the centrally departed any more than the obituarist. It was just so with Harvey

Contractor. The reports had professional finesse but lacked true knowledge. Bognor knew both rather better than the back of his hand. Which was why he eliminated them from his enquiries.

SIX

Sir Simon and Lady Bognor went for a walk later that morning, before the sherry which always preceded Sunday lunch.

The two had walked together since before they were married and it had become a ritual, even though their walking had an imbalance which handicapped the process from the very beginning. This lay in the fact that Monica had two speeds and her husband only one. Never the twain did meet. Monica moved fast or slow. The former was designed for getting from A to B with maximum expedition and was used in airports, railway stations and other places of no passing interest, where the arriving was all that mattered and the travelling merely a tiresome necessity. The other, slower, speed was for window shopping. Bognor referred to it as dawdling.

He himself walked at a speed which suited him but, essentially, belonged to no one else. Because of this, he was often an anthropomorphism of Rudyard Kipling's 'cat that walked by himself'. He was at one and the same time gregarious and solitary, and his walking speed suited him. When it was appropriate he adjusted his speed to that of other people, but he was basically only happy at his own idiosyncratic medium pace. It left him alone with his own thoughts, untroubled by interruption.

So Simon and Monica walked at different speeds, but they sang from the same, or at least similar, hymn sheets and talked the same game. Since they had first met, they had been each other's greatest, usually only, confidants. They talked together often and in different situations, many stationary, but they had always talked together *en plein air*, walking. This involved compromise and usually meant that Simon walked faster or slower than he would have liked. If he maintained his own pace, he usually fell behind his wife or pulled ahead. In either case, conversation became impossible. Sometimes this worked.

Today, however, was a talking occasion taken at a slow speed, which meant that Bognor took his foot off the gas pedal and sauntered alongside his wife, concentrating on her but also appreciating the wild garlic.

'I don't believe the vicar killed himself,' he began, as they left the ha-ha behind them and turned right into the woodland garden.

'Why not?' Monica wanted to know. 'Are you quite sure it's not because that unpleasant chief constable thinks otherwise?'

Bognor wondered whether the cowpat he had rather adroitly avoided was actually cow dung or belonged to some other animal; wilder and more obviously suited to woodland rather than open pasture or meadow. She could be right. He had a knee-jerk objection to authoritarianism, particularly when it was based on convenience rather than true authority. If men like Jones took a view then Bognor's immediate response was to take another, preferably contrary. He had learned to disguise this with a fog of bureaucratic prevarication which made him seem more amenable and reasonable than he actually was. He never fooled himself, and seldom Monica, but he was surprisingly good at pulling the wool over the eyes. Better still, he was a past master at making people think that if wool had been pulled, it was they and not Bognor who had done the pulling.

'You're quite right,' he conceded. 'I don't like the chief constable and I'm inclined to disagree with whatever he says. On the other hand, I really don't think the Reverend Sebastian Fludd dunnit.'

'Why not?' his wife wanted to know.

Bognor did some more thinking and then said, 'Because it's simply not in character. He wasn't a natural suicide.'

'No such thing,' said Monica. She spoke with certainty laced with a touch of asperity. 'The oddest and least likely people kill themselves, often for the most absurd and least predictable reasons. You know that. You've seen it often enough.'

This was true. They both knew it. They had both experienced examples.

'Even so,' said Bognor, in what to anyone else might have seemed a lame remark.

'Don't tell me,' said Monica. 'You feel it. Deep down.' She acknowledged this sixth sense of his and recognized that it was what distinguished the great from the mundane. Methodology got you so far but proceeding by the book was, in her eyes, the mark of the second-rate. Anyone could read a book, assimilate the essential message it contained and then proceed accordingly. It took something akin to genius to break rules, ignore convention and not to pay too much attention to what the book said.

Both of them believed this with a consuming and unifying passion. Moulds were made to be thrown out; rules and laws led to repetition and rote. Gut instinct was what marked men out. Mozart and Shakespeare and Leonardo da Vinci were great because they dared to do things differently; those who followed were second-rate because they did the same.

'If he didn't do it, then who did?' Monica asked, pertinently enough.

'The wife found him,' said Bognor. 'She was the nearest.'

'But was she the dearest?' she asked.

'Aha,' said Bognor, stepping over more dung. The countryside was full of excrement. This looked like some sort of deer muck. Not domestic dung, despite its neat identical rows of brown pellets. Orderly ordure. 'Good point. It sounds like a basically antiseptic union.'

'Not like some,' she said.

'Maybe not,' he said, refusing to rise to such obvious bait, even on a Sunday morning in the country.

'Leaving motive on one side for the time being,' said Monica, 'she had the opportunity.'

'So we're saying that she followed her husband into his church, interrupted his sermon-prep, made him tie a rope round his neck, attached it to a beam, stood him on a suitable chair and then kicked it away, causing him to suffocate, or whatever.'

'We're not saying that,' said Monica.

'No,' conceded her husband, 'but if we're suggesting that Mrs Fludd murdered her husband, then something along those lines must have happened. Why be so melodramatic? Why not just put something lethal in his Ovaltine one night at the rectory?'

'Because if she did that, dummy, she would have been the only suspect. By topping the unfortunate Sebastian in church, she created a whole raft of other possibilities and other suspects. She deflected attention, made herself just one among many, rather than the only possibility. It's obvious.'

This was unanswerable. Bognor remained silent. Finally, he said, 'So if she did it, she was being cold-blooded enough to finger other suspects.'

'If it was her,' said Monica, 'it was cold-blooded. No getting away from that.'

'If it was her,' said Bognor, 'it would have to be a persuasion job. She wouldn't have had the strength to do all the preliminary business, even if she could have kicked the chair away from under him. If it were her, then it would be amazingly cold-blooded and preconceived in every possible way. I'm not sure anyone is that calculating.'

'Oh yes, they are,' said Monica. 'You know the old saw: divorce no, murder yes. Catholics say it mostly. Maybe Mrs Fludd was like that.'

'So, Mrs Fludd would rather have killed her husband than divorce him. If she wanted to end the relationship then she had no option. Death or nothing. She might offend the law of the land but not of God.'

'You're twisting what I said,' Monica protested. 'Besides killing people is wrong. There's a commandment about it. God sent the word down from the mountain on a tablet. Via Moses. It was a serious old testament prophet job.'

'A bitter pill for some to swallow.' Bognor grinned. There were moments when he loved his wife very much. This was one of them. They had learned to tolerate each other's feeble jokes. He inhaled the smells of the countryside and reflected that there were worse things for a man to be doing before Sunday lunch than going for a walk in rural parkland. Even when death loomed so large in the immediate background. After all, death was part of his job, and if they couldn't both accept that, then they could accept nothing. In the long run, they were all dead and death provided interesting and crucial conundra. He was glad that his job involved basics and not peripherals.

'For what it's worth, I don't think the reverend was the victim of a nuptial murder, but at this stage I don't want to rule anyone out. Not even Mrs Fludd.'

'But if it wasn't Mrs Fludd . . . mind your feet . . . it was someone who knew the vicar's movements. They knew he'd be in church preparing his sermon.'

'Unless they had an appointment. Sebastian might have arranged a meeting with his killer.'

'That sounds unduly defeatist,' complained Monica. 'We're not talking euthanasia here. I don't see any evidence for the reverend wanting himself dead.'

'I don't mean that he knew the killer was his killer,' said Bognor, not adding the word 'stupid', though his tone implied it. 'But if he was murdered by someone he thought he could trust, someone he believed was a friend, then there's no reason why he shouldn't have made an appointment with him.'

'Or her.' His wife was a stickler for feminine equality, even when it was a question of murder suspects. He admired her for it.

'You think it might have been a woman?'

She thought for a moment, as if the idea had only just occurred to her.

'I don't see why not,' she said. 'The only possible reason for supposing it was a man that did it is if it's a question of brute strength. I'm prepared to concede that the average man is stronger than the average woman. But we aren't talking brute strength here.'

'Big of you.' His wife's feminism was a matter of edgy humour between them. Deep down, Bognor reckoned he was more of a feminist than she was; Monica, on the other hand, tended to the Marilyn French view that all men were rapists no matter what. Unsurprisingly, they both took considerable exception to such opposing views in the battle of the sexes, so that they went unexpressed, even though they were at the root of all arguments on matters of gender. Part of the problem was that husband and wife both regarded themselves as liberal and progressive on matters of sex, whereas in fact they were as susceptible to ingrained prejudice as the next man or woman. In professional matters this signified little, but they suffered from the popular belief that they were both in their quite different ways superior to the normal conventions that applied to the essential differences between men and women. In fact, they suffered from the usual old-fashioned failings that had afflicted men and women for ever. Bognor, for example, did not really see the point in soap and water; Monica, however, could not have too much of either. There were other differences involving everything from map reading, through punctuality, to shopping for shoes. Both would hotly deny that they ever succumbed to sexual stereotyping. Neither, however, would be entirely correct.

Privately, Bognor thought women made rotten detectives and, if forced to admit it, he would have included his wife in that generalization. Monica, more or less, up to a point, thought precisely the opposite.

But neither of them would ever admit it.

'I feel like a dry sherry,' he said, looking, like all Englishman, at his watch whenever the question of alcoholic drink was mentioned.

'G and T for me,' she said, 'and an olive from Fortnums. One thing I'll say for your old friend, he does Bombay Sapphire and a mean olive.'

And they turned for the ha-ha and home, with nothing resolved and the mysterious death of the vicar still hovering uneasily on what was otherwise a perfect country Sunday. They both enjoyed habit, particularly when it blurred into tradition. There was something comforting about the sort of library drinks, decent but unfussy meat and two veg with a claret to match and a couple of Labradors under the table. It may not have made Britain Great but it certainly made England English.

Even a murdered vicar had an agreeably timeless feel to it. One felt the English had been murdering vicars and drinking warm sherry since time immemorial. Rooks cawed as they negotiated the cattle grid on to the gravel and lawn, which led up to an Englishman's cockeyed version of what Palladio had built for the nobility of the Veneto. It was like so many things English – a friendly, agreeable, slightly tumbledown misunderstanding of the real thing. England was meant to be frayed at the edges, well worn and a not quite perfect fit.

Even sudden death had an old banger, rust-bucket feel to it. That was the British way of murder that was.

SEVEN

One of the forensic pleasures of weekends chez Fludd was working out the antecedents of the principle component of the main course at Sunday lunch. Sometimes, it was so difficult to be sure, that there was argument about whether this was fish, fowl or something furry. In fairness to the kitchen, it had to be admitted that it was usually possible to eliminate chicken and fish which seldom featured on Sundays anyway. (There had been a memorable occasion when they had been completely foxed by some pheasant masquerading as something completely different.)

The Bognors couldn't agree on whether the blame was Mrs Brandon's or Lady Fludd's. The problem lay in the habit of roasting the meat the night before serving, carving it into servable slices, and then dousing it in gravy and reheating in time for Sunday lunch. It was invariably double-over-cooked and grey in colour, blotting paper in taste. This was a well-established custom in a certain sort of traditional country house. It had everything to do with convenience and nothing whatever to do with gastronomy.

From a Julia Child, Elizabeth David, or celebrity chef point of view, Sunday lunch at the Fludds had nothing to recommend it, but for a semi-professional nostalgic, such as Sir Simon, it had a lot going for it. This was how life used to be when he was growing up. It didn't taste of much but it was the same for everyone; equality of nothing very much. It was a bit like the former East Germany, for which he had a sneaking regard. Nobody had anything much better than a lawnmower masquerading as a motor car; you all lived off a hundred and one ways with wurst and dumplings; but on the other hand everyone had beer and jobs. Also, in a curious way, each other. The older and grander Bognor became, the more he believed in society, in pulling together and being kind to one's neighbours. Consumerism, conspicuous consumption and celebrity seemed to involve competition of a sort he could not relish. He liked the quiet contemplative life and did not much care for kicking sand in the face of the people who lived next door.

Thus Sunday lunch with the Fludds. It was an oddly relaxing meal, familiar, unflashy and sound in an old-fashioned way that had gone out of favour, along with tweed, leather and shaving brushes made from badger bristle. There were more efficient, and indeed more enjoyable, ways of eating but he took pleasure in Sunday lunch at the Fludds not because of the food and drink, but despite them.

'Tiresome,' said Sir Branwell, carving something which had probably once been a bird. There was evidence of wings. 'If one is going to be murdered there is a time and place. Immediately before the festival is not one of them. And who in his right mind would want to kill the Reverend Sebastian? Sebby would never hurt a fly.'

'Who said anything about their right mind?' enquired Lady Bognor, watching the dissection with apprehension.

'The point I am making is that Sebby's death is "tiresome". I simply don't believe any other word will do.'

The point Sir Branwell was actually making was that any event which interfered with the world as he knew it was inappropriate. Although he would deny that he had actually created that world, it was the one which he had inherited and with which he felt comfortable. He was not the fourteenth baronet for nothing, but even if he was he enjoyed the tidy, predictable society in which he found himself, and did not like it being compromised by murder or even accidental death. Life for Sir Branwell and his ilk was convenient or it was nothing. Murder was inconvenient.

This was the whole point of sudden death. For a certain sort of Englishman, it lacked drama and excitement, and definitely such emotions as grief or upset of an essentially trivial nature. Grief, unless one's dogs or horses were involved, was alien to Sir Branwell and men like him, of whom there were a surprisingly large number. Maybe that was why the majority of British crime fiction was so anodyne and bloodless. Perhaps it was the fault of all those middle-class Dames – from Agatha Christie to Phyllis James. Not that Bognor had anything but admiration for these formid-able ladies, but he wasn't altogether sure that they had done a lot for murder most foul. In their hands, it wasn't as foul as it was in real life.

Except that for Sir Branwell, it wasn't.

'Inconvenient, very,' he said. 'If he wanted to top himself, he could surely have waited until after the festival, not to mention his sermon.'

'If he did kill himself – which seems improbable – then the balance of his mind would have been disturbed, which in turn would have meant that he didn't give a flying whatsit for the festival or his sermon. Hard to believe but true nonetheless.' This from Lady Bognor. As always, he thought to himself, the still shrill voice of reason, and yet reason and common sense were strangely inapplicable at times like this. This was what was so often wrong with the English murder. It had become a middle-class affair: sanitized; rendered prim. Even the traditional English funeral – of the sort the Reverend Sebastian would soon enjoy – took place with a closed wooden box. There was no public burning of the body, no eating by vultures, no sense of the catastrophe of death. It was all neat, tidy, orderly, and part of the warp and weft Agatha Christie and the other women had a lot to answer for.

'What Monica means is that it's all a bit of a shambles,' he found himself saying. 'Of course it's inconvenient. Dashed inconvenient, you could say, but murder's like that. Messy.'

Monica gave him one of her looks, in which affection and exasperation were mixed in equal measure, but she said nothing.

'All I can say,' said Sir Branwell, handing round plates of charred bird, 'is that mess is for other people. I don't do mess. As you should well know, Simon.'

This was perfectly true. Even at Apocrypha, Fludd had

been remarkable for his fastidiousness. In an untidy world, he was almost impossibly neat. Even when vomiting after drink, he always managed to make an excuse and find the loo, causing as little trouble as possible. He was like that. '*Noblesse*,' he said, rather too often, '*oblige*.'

'We'll try to reduce the mess,' said Bognor, sounding pompous, aware of the fact, but unable to see a way of seeming otherwise, 'that's our job. Or part of it. Lucky that we were here. On the other hand, a very important part of my job is to see that justice is done. And seen to be done.'

The pomposity was on overload. He knew this but could think of no way of diminishing it.

'Bugger justice!' said his host, doing it for him.

The roast bird was barely edible and defied identification. Down under it would probably have been roadkill, but in England it was more likely to be Fluddkill, brought down by the squire's ancient Purdey twelve-bore. The pudding was equally themeless, though it was steamed and came with custard. You didn't dine at Casa Fludd on account of what the baronet insisted on calling 'scoff', although he kept a decent cellar and served perfectly acceptable claret to accompany the execrable food.

Conversation continued to focus on the death of the Reverend Sebastian, but was procedural rather than forensic. The wives did not have particularly strong opinions for once and were, on the whole, content to take their husbands' side. This was unusual, as was the men's diametrically opposed opinion. They usually agreed, if only to differ, but, faced with the death of the vicar, they took up very decided positions on either side of the fence.

Sir Branwell was all for tidiness, Bognor for solving the puzzle. Time was when Simon might have agreed with the need for order, but age had not wearied him, nor the years condemned. Instead, he had become zealous in the pursuit of truth. Sir Branwell, on the other hand, was all for truth, provided it didn't get in the way.

Their disagreement was profound but polite. They had been friends for ever and differences of opinion could not

change that. Neither of them wished it. When the apology
of a pudding had been cleared away, coffee – weak and
tepid – appeared in a pot, along with minute cups, and a
carafe of acceptable port began to circulate steadily among
the four of them.

It was ever thus.

'No question of cancelling the festival?' asked Bognor.

'Good grief, no,' said his host, slurping port like the late
Keith Floyd, whom in some respects he resembled.

'Sebastian wouldn't have wished it,' said his hostess with
enviable certainty. 'He would have wanted the show to go
on.'

'Then why kill himself?' asked Lady Bognor, going to
the heart of the matter with predictable shrewdness.

'That's why I think someone else did him in,' said Bognor.
'The late Reverend was not a boat-rocker. He wouldn't have
thrown the entire event into jeopardy, even if he were
depressed.'

'I don't want bloody journalists sniffing around,' said Sir
Branwell. He pronounced the offending word 'jawnalists',
as in 'jaw-jaw, not war-war'. He didn't like the press, referring with contempt to 'that little creep Evans' and 'that
foreign republican Murdoch'. The Bognors agreed in the
particular, but not the general. They were for a free press,
which, in general terms, they felt the British no longer had.
Discuss.

'You and I are always going to see things differently. If
someone killed the reverend, then that's wrong, and they
should be made to pay for it.'

'Won't bring him back though,' said Fludd, not unreason-
ably, 'and trying to find the murderer is going to break a
whole nest of eggs without, as it were, making an edible
omelette.'

'Brannie's right,' said Lady Fludd. 'A whole lot of journalists crawling all over the place, smuggling themselves into
the house in laundry baskets, lives exposed to ridicule or
worse, coals raked over, and to no avail whatever. Absolutely
no avail whatever.'

'Quite,' said her husband.

The port circulated.

'Not necessarily,' said Bognor.

'Not necessarily what?' countered Fludd, in the manner of an Apocrypha tutor picking up a woolly argument and exposing it for the moth-eaten cardigan it really was.

'Avail,' said Bognor. 'Not necessarily to no avail. The truth availeth and all that. I'm not saying the process will be easy, or even pleasant. These things seldom are. But at the end of the day, we will have a result. Nothing will have been swept under the carpet.'

'I rather resent the idea that I am sweeping Sebastian under the carpet. I am letting him rest in peace, as he so plainly wished.'

'I'm not sure that's what the vicar would have wished. If someone else killed him, then he certainly didn't. If you really want to know, I think that's as good a proof as anything that he was murdered. If it were suicide, he'd have chosen almost any other day of the year. He certainly wouldn't have created a vacuum at the beginning of the festival.'

'I still think we should avoid undue fuss,' said Sir Branwell.

'We don't do fuss,' said his wife. They didn't, either. It was something that Hitler and other would-be invaders didn't understand about a certain sort of Briton. You didn't mess with people like the Fludds. They did team teas for the cricket, commanded the Home Guard and didn't do fuss. Period. Not to be roused. Slow to be so, but dangerous when done. An ancient cliché, but true nonetheless.

'I think,' said Bognor, glaring at his port, 'that I should visit the scene of the crime. You never know what the conventional people may have missed.'

'We'd all feel happier,' said Lady Fludd, 'if we thought everything was in your hands and could be handled by someone like you. Without, you know, fuss.'

'Quite,' said Sir Simon. 'Safe pair of hands.'

His wife would have rolled her eyes under some circumstances, but obviously felt such a gesture was inappropriate in this time and in this company.

'Church,' she said. 'Simon and I had better have a sniff round St Teath's or whatever. A smell and a bell. Who knows?'

'It's locked,' said Sir Branwell, 'but I have a key.'

EIGHT

C hurch was a church was a church. Also a scene of crime. Parts of it had been sectioned off with fluo-rescent tape. Two police officers were on guard. They too were dressed fluorescently. Fluorescence was all the rage these days, thought Bognor whimsically. It was the new luminous orange. It conveyed authority. Confronted with fluorescence, people became orderly. They formed queues, deferred, asked no questions, told no lies. Better a fluorescent jacket than a knighthood. He should know.

'Cold in here,' said Monica, shivering. It wasn't really, but it felt like it. Scenes of crime, which meant places where murder had been committed, often felt colder than they actually were. Association of ideas, fact of life. Or death.

Bognor didn't know what he was looking for. He seldom did. This mattered very little. In fact, knowing exactly what one was looking for was often a drawback, because it indicated a closed mind incapable of assimilating the unexpected and dealing with surprise. And murder was nearly always a tale of the unexpected, a guilty thing surprised.

He gazed about him, looking for anything that was out of place and not as it should be. Above the pulpit, the board advertised hymns. There were four of them numbered, all to be found in *Hymns Ancient and Modern*. Nothing out of order there, but, even so, he felt he should see what the choir and congregation had been scheduled to sing.

The result was surprising. Christmas carols, harvest thanksgivings, wedding celebrations and deferential thanks for the graciousness of the royal family were all very well in their way, but not at this time of year, and not all together at once. It probably didn't signify, but it was still unexpected. He was reminded of the biblical clues in the Stieg Larsson whodunnit about the girl with the tattoo and of the clues in Dan Brown's best-seller. Both had been read by millions, and there was no reason to suppose that an avid reader had not taken the idea and played with it when killing the Rector of Mallborne.

On the other hand, it could be that Sir Teath's was a more than usually catholic church, and the selection of hymns was more than usually wide. After all, the bishop was Ebenezer Lariat, aka Bishop Ebb, an old friend of Simon's ever since they had worked together on the great communion wine scandal of 1983. He was now Bishop of Lymington, and was standing in at short notice for the Reverend Sebastian on the grounds that he was the late Rev.'s superior and could also deliver fifteen or so plausible sermonic minutes at the drop of a mitre. Alas, no room for debutants, even ones as keen as Simon.

Bishop Ebb was due in an hour or so.

The bishop was an Oxford man too. Keble, and muscular with it. He was a rowing blue, and Bognor could picture him in a pink Leander cap, much too small for him, on a foggy, damp boat-race day. He took a third class honours degree in Geography, and was into broken glass and hearty pursuits rather than religion. That came later.

Cuddesdon, curacy in the industrial north, a living in the south, and a doubtful sexuality, coupled with an understated interest in choir boys and wolf cubs, added up to a more or less conventional path to episcopacy. That, at least, was what Contractor thought, and Bognor was inclined to agree.

Ebenezer was not stupid, but he was, on the whole, lazy and had risen, if not exactly without trace, without apparently troubling the scorers. For a relatively public figure, he maintained a low, virtually private, profile. He had published a non-controversial treatise on prayer, aimed, characteristically, at a wide and relatively unspecific audience. This had sold solidly rather than spectacularly, and was eclipsed by his reworking of *Hymns Ancient and Modern* with a fashionable and predictable emphasis on the Modern.

Bognor forgot where he had first met him, but he seemed to have been part of his emotional scenery for as long as he could remember. From time to time, he consulted Ebenezer on church matters, and he always asked him to their annual Christmas party, if only as a token cleric. Monica didn't care for him – a usual lack of liking for her sex, though this was by no means universal. The bishop had a very loyal cook and housekeeper called Mrs Grimes. There may have been a Mr Grimes, but, even if he had once existed, he was long departed.

As far as religiosity was concerned, Lariat-Lymington was all things to most men. He was generally considered 'sound', but no one knew (or, to be truthful, much cared) where exactly he stood on the ordination of women, whether he was a closet Catholic, or if he thought that the Church of England at prayer, flower-arranging, or even holy dusting, was in any way significant. The bishop just 'was'.

It was not like Contractor to fail in a task, and he would argue persuasively that, as far as Ebenezer was concerned, he had done the job. Nevertheless, there was a phrase that Bognor had learned from a friend who had become some sort of journalist. This was 'We do not feel the character quite comes alive'. This was normally the prelude to a rejection in the politest possible sense. Everything was there: education, sporting achievements, size of hat and shoes, colour of eyes, maiden name of maiden aunt, but somehow the Rt Rev. Ebenezer remained strangely skeletal. For all his assiduity and perspicacity, Contractor had failed to put blood and flesh on the bare bones. The bishop remained elusively skeletal. He remained so to all inquisitors, leading some sceptics to maintain that, when you stripped away the flummery and the frocks, the cope and cape, the crook and mitre, there was nothing there at all.

Perhaps so, perhaps not. Despite the sonorous public performance (the bishop had a deep baritone voice, with a matching delivery, of which he was inordinately proud), Ebenezer was a bit of a footnote. Maybe not even that. Which did not mean that he did not possess hidden depths or lacked the capacity to kill.

Meanwhile, Bognor cogitated. He noted the numbers on the hymn board and the words which matched them in *Hymns Ancient and Modern*. He had no Bible with him, but would borrow one later and cudgel the grey matter yet further in the hope of elucidation. He stared long and hard at the spot above which the cleric's limp body had recently hung, but, try as he might, his staring produced no answers.

Conceding surrender, if only temporarily, he shifted to seek the woman. However, the only woman who seemed to fit any bill at all was Dorcas Fludd, wife of the Reverend Sebastian, and even he was compelled to admit that Dorcas was a very dark horse indeed. *Cherchez* Dorcas was an unproductive idea, and yet she and the reverend had been man and wife. They must once, unappealing though the idea might seem, have fancied each other and even, despite the lack of children, had carnal knowledge of each other. And Dorcas was a decent enough sort. Just not what you might call sexy.

You couldn't, on reflection, rule Dorcas out of the equation. Just because you didn't fancy her, just because most of the world didn't fancy her, didn't mean that she couldn't kindle fierce passions in the odd, and he meant odd, breast.

He would have to have a word with her, in the hope of finding out what made her and Sebastian tick. It was she who had discovered him, she who had come straight to his cousins, she who had seemed so distraught. Alas, poor sausage!

Bognor was not a particularly religious man. Lapsed C of E, like most of those brought up in the faith. Nevertheless, he had a vestigial respect for the noise it made and for matins and evensong, for the creed, for psalms, hymns and that curious wheedling, sonorous vicar's voice, which seemed such an essential adjunct to that conventional middle-of-the-road, essentially bloodless faith. It was like English murder, like, in fact, so much of English life: ordered, tidy, neat, devoid of passion. The Church of England queued. The Church of England did not step out of line. The Church of England knew its place. Like so many English things, it was oddly lapsed and in an apparent state of abeyance, and yet there was a sense in which it was slumbering, not dead, and, to men like Bognor, still commanded respect, even at times a certain dread.

He found himself reflecting thus, as he stood in St Teath's

that day. He was in the presence of death, and he felt it. The sense of doom and finality was visceral, and was enhanced by his surroundings. It didn't matter that the Church, which used to be so central, had grown peripheral and unimportant. It had, for years, been a vital part of being a person. One was christened in church, one was married in church, one's funeral was held in church. It marked one's beginning and one's end, and also, more importantly, it was part of one's routine. Even in Bognor's childhood, it had been a regular Sunday ritual, and in childhood the day had begun and ended with prayers. In the morning, it was school chapels, and in the evening, it tended to be smaller house dining rooms. But it was a part of life, as essential a part as anything, and even though he, like so many, had lapsed, it remained with him for ever and he respected, sometimes loved, the noise it made.

The fact that the dead man was ordained and had died in his own church, gave the whole event a majesty that would otherwise have been lacking, even though Sir Branwell found the mystery an affront to his sense of order and tidiness, rather than something apocalyptic. One would have thought that Bognor, much of whose business was death and who dealt with it most days of his life, would have become inured to the whole idea. Instead of that, however, it was he who was still in awe of the end of life, and men like Sir Branwell who regarded it essentially as a tiresome disruption of routine. Sir Branwell and Lady Fludd had never even seen a dead body. The same was true of most English people of their generation. It was lack of familiarity which bred contempt. Familiarity induced awe, respect and fear. It made Bognor fanatical about truth and justice, and led him to do his best to eradicate murder from the vocabulary. For most people, death was little more than an inconvenience. Bognor was a traditionalist in such matters.

He was reflecting on conservatism, mortality and meaning, when he sensed movement behind him and realized that Bishop Ebb had arrived early. He was wearing grey flannel bags, a tweed jacket along with a purple vest, and an enormous and showily bling pectoral cross.

'Well,' said the bishop, 'he moves in mysterious ways his wonders to perform. I hadn't intended to be here until I got Branwell's SOS, but now our paths cross once more. You're the silver lining to a deep black cloud. Welcome to St Teath's.'

And he shook Bognor by the hand. Warmly. Bognor had experienced enough cool handshakes in his life to recognize the difference. The bishop smiled with his eyes too, and he exuded warmth. Some, possibly even most, episcopal personages were cold to the point of cadaverousness, but not Ebenezer Lymington. You wanted to snuggle up to him and bask.

'Nice to see you, Bishop,' said Bognor. 'Sorry about the circumstances, but still good to see you around.'

It was indeed good to have a senior man of God around, and one who could not possibly be a suspect. No Reverend Green, no lead piping in the library, no spanner in the conservatory. Colonel Mustard, Miss Scarlet, Professor Plum: all possible. But not Bishop Ebb. His alibi was perfect, quite apart from the fact that he was far too saintly. Loren Estelman or Sarah Paretsky might have had a killer prelate in the mean streets of Detroit or Chicago, but no such person would disfigure the pages of a mystery set in rural England. The bishop didn't do it. And in England, couldn't. Not so elsewhere.

'So, penny for your thoughts,' said the Rt Rev. Ebenezer. 'Our friend the Lord Lieutenant would have us believe that Sebastian killed himself. He could be right, even if his reasons are wrong. It wouldn't be the first time that's happened. Sir Branwell doesn't like anything to interfere with the status quo, but, in my experience, life and death aren't like that. They say that God's joke is men making plans for the future. There's a lot in that. I have predicated my life on the notion that tomorrow is an illusion and that one is constantly taken by surprise. It's the only way to retain a semblance of control. Branwell believes that if you talk slowly and loudly enough, everything will pan out according to his wishes.'

'And sometimes that happens,' said Bognor.

'That's what I mean about being right for the wrong reasons,' said the bishop. 'It all comes down to God moving in mysterious ways his wonders to perform. They *are* wonders, He *is* mysterious. That's part of the point. If it was all clear-cut and logical, we'd all be like Dawkins, which would be very boring.'

'Up to a point,' he said.

The bishop ignored this.

'Like you,' he said, 'I'd like to see a result, and the right one as well. I don't happen to think Sebastian killed himself. But there you go. I also don't believe in sweeping things under the carpet. My God is a messy God. It's one of the reasons I worship him.'

He paused. Bognor reflected that he liked the bishop.

'Christianity,' continued His Grace, 'requires an act of faith. An awful lot of people, on both sides of the fence, don't understand this. If it were a question of logic, none of us would be Christians. It doesn't make what we laughingly call "sense". That's why we talk about "faith" and "belief". You have to have one and suspend the other, if you're going to belong to the church.'

'Then why,' asked Bognor, who tended to just such an irrational subscription to the established church, 'do so many churchmen, prelates such as you, try to justify Christianity as if it were, well, defensible?'

Bishop Ebb rolled his eyes and splayed his hands.

'That's their decision!' he said. 'I think they play into the hands of atheists and agnostics, but there you are. It's up to them. I believe that belief requires a leap of faith.'

'I see,' said Bognor, not seeing anything at all, but feeling that some sort of vision was expected.

'And it was a leap that poor dead Sebastian was finding increasingly difficult.'

'*Really?*'

'Yes, really. We'd discussed the matter several times in the last few weeks and months. Sebastian was concerned that he was losing his vocation.' The bishop sighed. 'Which is one reason why I am retaining an open mind on the subject of his death. Suicide for a man of the cloth is particularly dreadful. So's loss of faith for an ordained minister. Bad enough for anyone, but, for someone in Sebastian's position, a particularly difficult – and lonely place – in which to be.'

'He shouldn't have been lonely. There was you, his flock, his wife.'

'Alas, poor Dorcas!' said the bishop in sepulchral tones, accompanied by the eye-rolling, both of which Bognor was beginning to find a touch irritating, fond of Ebenezer though he was.

'Why "poor Dorcas"?' asked Bognor, wondering if he was right to follow the advice about searching for the *femme*, if the *femme* was Dorcas, or whether there was another *femme* involved. *Fatale*, presumably.

'Let us just say,' said Ebenezer Lariat, 'that Sebastian's relationship with his wife was deteriorating as rapidly as that with his Lord and Master.'

Bognor said nothing. There was nothing much to say. Internally, however, cogs were whirring.

NINE

The Bognors' bedroom belonged to another era. It was enormous, and the bed was a four-poster, which needed the hot-water bottles scrupulously filled and inserted under the sheets every night by Peggoty Brandon. The walls were hung with pictures to do with hunting and the Fludds – caricatures of previous baronets in the manner of Spy, with Fludds in pink, dogs lolloping along with tongues hanging out, jovial looking men on horseback, and the occasional fox, glimpsed from afar. The central heating existed, but was ancient and perfunctory, the windows leaked and there was a damp patch on the ceiling and a bucket on the floor. The patch grew wetter in bad weather and the bucket filled. There were two high-backed Victorian armchairs on either side of the fire, which was always laid and sometimes lit. There was a bottle of Malvern water and two glasses, also, because the Bognors were the Bognors and the Fludds the Fludds, a decanter of Scotch. This was not normally provided for guests; the Malvern water was.

The Bognors enjoyed the room, which was the one in which they always stayed. They were used to it and it suited them. Very occasionally, when the Fludds opened the house and gardens for charity – usually the Red Cross or the Army Benevolent Fund – the four-poster was roped off behind a plush bell-pull of a barricade kept for such occasions, but more often it was a private sanctuary for the Bognors, penetrated only by the Brandons, apart from themselves.

This was where they retreated for the obligatory 'forty winks' which broke up the afternoon.

'The bishop turned up,' Bognor told his wife, who was already ten winks ahead of him.

'What, old Ebb?' Monica wanted to know.

'Yes. He was quite interesting about the deceased.'

'How so?'

Bognor told her about Fludd's loss of faith and loss of Dorcas.

'Reciprocated?' she asked.

'My sense is that the Lord still considered him one of his anointed, even if He felt a bit let down. Dorcas, on the other hand, was still fond of him. Not nutty or passionate, but that isn't, wasn't, in Dorcas's nature.'

'I'd feel a bit let down if one of my servants stopped believing in me. Imagine how Branwell and Camilla would feel if the Brandons suddenly said they didn't believe in them any more.'

'That's silly,' said Bognor.

'Not really,' said his wife. 'If the Lord dunnit, then it was suicide. That's one of His ways of doing people in. Otherwise it's war, car crashes, tsunamis, earthquake, wind and fire.'

'That's silly too,' said Bognor, 'but probably not as silly as anything to do with Dorcas.'

They mused and agreed silently. Dorcas was not, on the face of it, the sort of woman you would kill for; nor did she strike one as a murderess.

Bognor told her about the hymn board. Her memory was more photographic than his and when he repeated the numbers he had written down, she frowned in recognition. They meant something to her even without the hymnal to refer to. And they didn't stack up for her, any more than they had for him. She would need to think about it. The mind would be cudgelled and in due course, which could be at any moment, she'd provide an answer. On past form, it would probably be more or less right and more or less helpful. It was what made them such a formidable team, despite appearances.

'I think I should start interviewing,' he said. 'Even if the interviews don't add up to anything, I have to be seen to be going through the motions in the same way as if the police were involved. Most police procedure is just a question of form. In that sense, Branwell is right. They just get in the way and create mess and muddle. Branwell likes order. The police create disorder under the pretence of restoring order. Farcical. Very often they move into situations that are perfectly regulated and create chaos. Fact of life.'

Monica didn't respond. She had heard this before. Many times. The fact that she agreed, didn't make it any more original. The world was full of well-meaning people who wanted to improve life but made things worse. This is what made it go round, though the system was inevitably flawed and the difference between success and failure marginal. Many of Bognor's most spectacular successes had been achieved by beating the system. Orthodoxy was almost by definition second-rate. He could not, sensibly, be accused of being unorthodox, even if it sometimes looked like it.

He would begin interviewing people. It was what one did. That, on the whole, was where the clues were. If he were a policeman and did things 'according to the book', whatever that was, he would have started with Dorcas Fludd. Dorcas was the next of kin; Dorcas had found the body when Sebastian didn't turn up for supper (macaroni cheese, tinned peaches, Ovaltine); Dorcas was the one who grieved most and she was – if the book were to be believed, though the book didn't actually exist, except as a symbol of the orthodoxy Bognor was anxious to repudiate – also the prime suspect. *Cherchez la femme*. For all sorts of reasons, she should have been first in his queue. 'I'm sorry to intrude, Mrs Fludd, at such a sad time as this – but if you wouldn't mind, there are just one or two questions I have to ask. Would you say, for example, that your husband was behaving in any way unnaturally in the moments before he . . . er . . . died?'

She would have answered his questions, sobbing quietly into a handkerchief and drinking a medicinal brandy in tearful gulps, because that was what one did when one's husband, the vicar, had been found dead, swinging gently from a rope in his church one evening, when he should have been preparing his sermon. Had Bognor been a conventional Plod, he would have listened sympathetically, taken notes, expressed his condolences in a weary, undertaker's manner, and gone on his way, none the wiser, but satisfied that he had, according to the book, behaved in the correct manner.

But Simon Bognor was not a conventional Plod and he did not believe in the book, any more than the Reverend Sebastian had, according to his bishop, believed in God. And Bognor knew the answers to all the questions that a conventional Plod would have put to the new widow. He knew that the deceased was troubled about matters matrimonial and professional; he knew that he had last been seen by Dorcas, Mrs Fludd, after he had drunk two cups of tea, eaten a slice of fruit cake, wiped his lips fastidiously and kissed his wife a last fond, but dutiful, farewell on both cheeks, but not the mouth, with lips puckered but pursed. He put the time of this last sighting at around five, and the discovery of the body at around seven. As near as dammit, though it hardly mattered.

The truth of the matter was that he knew much of what was easy and would be nailed down in a form which could be read out in court without fear of contradiction. That was the nature of conventional work. It existed mainly in order to cover the rear of the person carrying it out. 'The police arrived and were, as usual, extremely efficient' as one well-known British crime writer always insisted. This was true enough, but the concomitant truth was that they were always amazingly lacking in imagination. Luckily, most killers were similarly unhampered, so that the two were in a sense made for each other; the one discovered the other; and everyone was more or less happy. The taxpayer believed that he had received his due and the press connived at the deceit.

So for this, and other reasons, Bognor seceded to talk first to chef-patron Gunther Battenburg. The main excuse for doing so was that he was bored and did not want to be bored further, as well as possibly being embarrassed, by talking to Dorcas Fludd. She could come later, when he knew enough about her late husband and his demise to ask questions which did not come from some non-existent but constraining manual.

'I think I'm going to have a word with Battenburg at the Fludd Arms,' he said nonchalantly to Monica, adding equally nonchalantly, 'Would you like to come?' though this was not so much a question as a supplication, to which the anticipated answer was 'yes'.

Thus, they set off through the picturesque little town to the pub which Gunther had put on the *carte gastronomique*.

Gunther Battenburg was almost certainly not his real name, but this didn't matter much. It was a *nom de cuisine*. Had he used his real name, which was something along the lines of Ron or Fred or Bill, he would have been handicapped, just as he would have been if he had used his second name, which was Jones, Smith, Brown, White or something equally banal and British. Gunther Battenburg sounded German or Swiss, but more importantly 'foreign'. Even the most British chefs sounded as if they came from somewhere else: Stein sounded Jewish, Ramsay Scottish and so on. There was always Delia and Elizabeth David, not to mention the Grigsons *mère et fille*, but Bognor always said they were exceptions that proved some rule or other, even if he wasn't sure what it was, or whether it was significant, or intended to convey even the most cursory obedience. The point was that Gunther Battenburg was not his real name, that everyone knew this, but that it didn't, in any important sense, make a blind bit of difference.

It was the same with the name of his establishment. To most of the world, his pub would always be the Fludd Arms, or The Fludd, but Gunther didn't believe that you would win Michelin stars with a place called the Fludd Arms, so he called it the Two by Two, instead. No one knew where the name came from, nor why he had chosen it, but it was the sort of name that won Michelin stars, and that was precisely what Gunther had achieved within a couple of years: one Michelin star, going on three.

The food at The Fludd used to be execrable, in the same way that Mrs Brandon's food at the manor used to be. Traditional English: meat and two veg, with the meat an indeterminate shade of grey and the veg boiled to within an inch of its life, if not beyond. Bread sauce with most things, especially sausage and birds. Puddings, mainly steamed for as long as possible, and served with Bird's custard, Tate and Lyle's Golden Syrup or jam. The jam was usually strawberry and commercially manufactured in a jar which used to have a label featuring golliwogs until they became outlawed under some legislation that said they would incite white people to hatred of black ones, possibly even make them murder them. The Bognors thought this unlikely, but shrugged and let it pass in an old-fashioned and ultimately rather dangerous British manner.

Bognor's young minion, Harvey Contractor, had obviously enjoyed his researches into the background of Gunther Battenburg. As Bognor had surmised, this was not his real name, nor German his nationality. He had been born around the Elephant and Castle, christened Frederick Micklewhite, some sort of cousin of the actor Michael Caine, another who had changed his name. Apparently, he had been having tea in some pseudo-swagger London hotel with his 'image consultant', who had told him that no celebrity chef could make it while named Micklewhite. 'Let me be cake,' said our man, parodying Marie Antoinette, but getting the third syllable wrong.

Battenburg and the deceased cleric had enjoyed a spectacular argument just two evenings before the crucial death. It had taken place at Gunther's restaurant when the vicar had come calling. The entire community, apart from the squire and his lady – the Bognors' host and hostess – seemed to know exactly what had happened, sentence by sentence, and, it seemed (though Battenburg denied fisticuffs), blow by blow. Sir Branwell, incidentally, resembled one of those old-fashioned pedagogues who claimed to know everything, while actually knowing nothing at all. The squire claimed to be omniscient and to have his finger on the pulse of the village. The reality was that the only person on whose person the squire's finger actually lay – and lightly at that – was his wife. And the same went for her. Maximum claim of intelligence, minimum basis in fact: the bane of bad security services everywhere.

The Reverend Sebastian Fludd had had a good idea. 'Good ideas' were frequently fatal in Bognor's view. They invariably seemed wonderful at the point of genesis, which was often the bath, but they almost always seemed less so at the point of delivery. It was also a mistake to start a conversation, particularly when one was the supplicant, with the words 'I have an idea'. It seemed to be acknow-ledged that this was how the vicar opened. It was not good. The equivalent of a feeble loosener or underarm lob. It cried out to be hit over a distant boundary or smashed for an immediate winner.

Battenburg, aka Micklewhite, duly obliged.

'I deal in food, not ideas,' he said. 'Recipes, maybe. Ideas are for boffins and buffoons.'

'My big idea is to have a foodless Christmas dinner, with all profits going to the starving millions around the world.'

'Bugger the starving millions,' said the chef pithily.

'I beg your pardon,' said the reverend.

'Granted,' said Gunther. 'My punters are paying a lot of money for their Christmas gourmet break. They expect some bang for their buck. Edible bang; drinkable bang; bang they can stuff in their gobs.'

From there on, the conversation had deteriorated, though whether or not words gave way to something more physical was a moot point.

At some point, apparently, Battenburg had threatened the vicar with death, though this was in dispute and vehemently denied by Battenburg, though affirmed by Dorcas Fludd who, needless to say, had evidence only at second-hand.

'I see,' said Bognor, finishing Contractor's report and staring into space. As usual, when he uttered these words, he saw nothing and, even if he did, he saw it through a glass, darkly.

There had obviously been a clash and it was inevitable. Battenburg relied on conspicuous consumption for his living; the reverend owed what little living he enjoyed to sackcloth and ashes. Battenburg owed his ease to rich people eating and drinking more than they should, without regard to any of the consequences. Fludd was the opposite. He would have been happier in a world without wealth, a world in which everyone starved, a world in which not only was Jack as good as his master, but all Jacks were sprats.

Bognor sighed. He could see the point of view of Mammon, aka Gluttony, and he could see the point of view of the ascetic who wanted everyone else to be in a state of similar self-denial. Fence-sitting was a hazard as far as he was concerned. This didn't mean that he was slow to apportion real blame and to find people guilty. Nor did it involve a suspension of prejudice. He was always on the side of indulgence and against abstinence. That didn't, however, make him unprofessional.

So, did he believe that the chef murdered the vicar? On balance, no. Chef Battenburg, in the heat of the moment, with a knife. Well, yes. Plausible. This, however, was a cold-blooded, premeditated crime and Battenberg did not seem that sort of person. Crime *de passion* in the heat of the kitchen, but not a murder in the still watches, in the presence of God. That was Bognor's feeling and, on the whole, his feelings served him well. They were not, however, infallible and while he was always careful to take them into account, he never allowed them to overrule ratiocination. So Battenburg could have done it. Of course he could. And he had a thoroughly plausible motive. Instinct said no, and the heart was often as reliable as the head.

Sir Branwell and Lady Fludd had only eaten at the Two by Two once since Battenburg took the place over and changed its name, but Sir Branwell pronounced it poncey and Camilla did not disagree. Not that the Fludds were unadventurous. They went abroad and ate well; the food at Sir Branwell's club was quietly ambitious and Sir Branwell quite enjoyed it. They particularly enjoyed Wilton's in Jermyn Street whenever a rich friend or relation took them there, but that didn't alter the fact that he found Gunther's food 'poncey'. It was a bit like changing one's kit at the Hogarth Roundabout. There was some stuff that one simply didn't eat on home turf, and Battenburg's came into that category. Likewise, the decor; though the cellar, despite new world additions, remained passable.

The chef was preparing snail porridge, the idea for which had been cribbed from his friend Heston Blumenthal, when the Bognors came calling.

Snail porridge was an unusual starter for the literary festival's inaugural supper, but it made a change from prawn cocktail, and it was, for many of the guests, acceptable and surprising.

Supper came after evensong and Sebastian's sermon. Snail porridge followed his grace. This year, His Grace, the Rt Rev. Ebenezer, would fill the gap, but meanwhile Bognor had some questions to ask the chef.

TEN

'Tell me, chef,' began Bognor, enjoying the cliché and wondering why Gunther was wearing a toque and check trousers, 'where were you yesterday, between the hours of five and seven?'

Gunther took off his toque, rubbed his eyes, and beamed at Lady Bognor.

'Would you care for a cup of something? Camomile tea? Herbal infusions? Or something a little stronger? A glass of prosecco, perhaps? I have a particularly fine one from a small estate in a village a few miles outside Verona. I have been buying from Guiseppe for several years.'

Monica said she'd like a glass of prosecco. She had learned recently that it was a sparkling wine in its own right, and not simply a cheaper Italian substitute for champagne. This was true, generally. Other people's sparkling whites were not just imitations of the French elixir, but wines with their own character. This was a lesson for life. People were not just inferior imitations of other people, but individuals in their own image. Same with chefs; same with Gunther. He wasn't just the next Heston Blumenthal – or a poor man's version of Heston – he was Gunther Battenburg. Or maybe not. But whoever he was, he existed in his own skin and he was his own man. There was no one quite like him.

Same with the Bognors. They were *sui generis*.

This was probably just as well, and it did not always seem thus to others. To Bognor, however, an element of nonconformity raised his best game.

'I always associate Battenberg with cake,' said Monica, puckering over her fizz. 'From a small town in Germany. Marzipan. Brightly coloured squares. Mildly embarrassing name for our own dear House of Windsor.'

'The cake is spelt with an "e" not a "u",' said Gunther.

'My name has little or nothing to do with the cake. *Hoffentlich.* I do not like cake in general, and I abhor this one in particular.'

'Like Vyvyans with a "y" in Cornwall, as opposed to an "i",' said Monica, ignoring her husband's fond but forbidding stare. He was warning her off, an admonition which the chef noticed and evidently respected.

'Prosit,' he said, raising his glass. 'I was here yesterday between the hours of five and seven, in answer to your question, Maestro. I was supervising prep for dinner. It is my custom.'

'We only have your word for that,' said Bognor beadily. Such scepticism was a stock-in-trade. He liked being thought of as a Maestro, though. He must use it in future. The flattery softened his response.

'I had my *batterie* here. You can ask them. They will vouch for my presence.'

'OK,' said Bognor, 'I have to ask questions such as this. Form's sake, you understand. Nothing sinister about them. They have to be asked, that's all. Busy night?'

Gunther looked thoughtful. '*Comme ci, comme ça,*' he said eventually. 'The first guests for the festival have arrived already. Brigadier Blenkinsop and his wife. Mademoiselle Book, the singer, and her friend. Maestro Allgood, the writer. They were all here.'

Bognor disliked Martin Allgood being referred to as 'maestro'. He had always thought of little Martin as a bit of a pipsqueak, and much disliked what little he had read of his. It didn't help that Monica seemed to a bit of a fan.

'All here already, so soon?'

Gunther nodded. There didn't seem to be anything to add, so a silence hung in the air, until it was broken by Bognor asking, 'The dead man. Did you know him?'

'The vicar? Of course. In a small community such as ours the vicar is a known person. Just like the squire, the person who runs the pub. And so on. There are not, I am told, as many vicars as once upon a time, and the Reverend Sebastian had other congregations and churches. He was busy. In former times, the vicar would perhaps not have been quite so busy but, alas, times have changed and the vicar today is a busy person.'

'You, however, are not a member of the Church of England?'

The chef seemed to think about this, but finally shook his head a little sadly.

'I was brought up as a Lutheran,' he said, 'but I am, as you say, "lapsed".' He laughed, as if pleased at having mastered such a difficult and essentially English concept. 'Lapsed,' he repeated. 'It is like your tea. It is weak, with much water.'

'Lapsang souchong,' said Monica, not helpfully.

The chef looked blank.

'So you knew the reverend as a pillar of the Establishment, rather than as a man of God?'

Gunther looked blanker yet. Maybe, thought Bognor, he really was foreign, and not a cookery school graduate from the East End of London.

'How well did you know the Reverend Sebastian?'

This time Gunther understood the question perfectly.

'He always said the grace at my festival dinner. Always the same words. "For what we are about to receive, may the Lord make us truly thankful." Quite dull. Always the same. Sir Branwell said that at school they had a joke toast which said "For baked beans and buttered toast, thank Father, Son and Holy Ghost", but I am not understanding the joke. Nor the reverend. He was very conservative. He liked to be thought, as you would say, "progressive", but he did not enjoy change. He enjoyed the same always: food, hymns, words, grace, women.'

'Women,' said Bognor, latching on to the oddity with speed. 'What makes you say women?'

Gunther Battenburg went pink.

'It is, as you say, a figure of speech.'

'But you thought the vicar was conservative when it came to sex?'

'Perhaps, but also, perhaps not.'

The chef was discomfited and Bognor pressed home his advantage.

'Sex,' he said. 'Would you describe yourself as conservative when it came to sex?'

Part of the fun of being a special investigator, even if only from the Board of Trade, was that it gave one a licence to ask questions from which one would normally have flinched. Thus sex.

'I'm sorry,' said Gunther, 'I am not understanding.'

Bognor was not sure where this was heading, but he asked the question that had been at the back of his mind long before he had actually met the chef.

'Gay are we, Gunther?'

Monica was obviously outraged at such an irrelevant intrusion.

'I hardly think . . .' she began, but her husband shushed her.

'Her Majesty's government doesn't pay for thought,' he said, 'especially from spouses. I just want to know whether Gunther here is homosexual.'

Gunther was no longer looking particularly pink.

'I don't understand what my sexual inclinations have to do with the death of the Reverend Sebastian,' he said, giving the impression of understanding perfectly. 'But, given a chance, I'll fuck anything that moves. Sex seldom comes into it.'

It wasn't clear whether the Bognors found the admission, or the use of the Anglo-Saxon word, the more upsetting. They belonged to a generation and a class which tended to believe that homosexuality was an unpleasant disease best not mentioned, and in which only out-and-out bounders, such as Peregrine Worsthorne, used four-letter words in public. Nevertheless, Bognor had asked the question. He should have been expecting an answer he didn't like and to hear words he only used, if at all, in private.

'You asked,' said the chef, after a longish pause. 'But I don't see how it is going to help poor Sebastian or nail his killer.'

'So you don't think it was suicide?'

'I didn't say that, but, on balance, I think it's unlikely. Sebastian was almost certainly gay, but I'd guess his sexuality was probably repressed.'

'What makes you say that?'

'I recognize the signs. Above all, only a certain sort of man would marry a woman like Dorcas, just as only a woman such as Dorcas would marry a gay cleric.'

'Meaning?'

'That Dorcas is a typical dyke. Repressed, non-practising, but still a dyke.'

Another silence.

'You feel it in your gut?'

'I feel it in my gut. More prosecco?'

The Bognors accepted and drank. In the old days, they would just have drunk with no questions asked. Nowadays, they had a problem. In today's world, everyone preferred it if one didn't drink alcohol at all. In any event, one was not allowed very much. The Bognors, however, belonged to a world and a generation which enjoyed a drink and did not regard this as a problem. Change of life. Bit like gaiety. What had once been a guilty secret was now an open affirmation.

'Anyway,' said Gunther, 'I didn't kill him. I don't know who did. I have a watertight alibi and no motive. May I go now and make porridge?'

Bognor glanced at his wife. She agreed, but no third party would have known. They took their glasses into what was, in former days, the snug, and was now all beige furniture and black and white photographs.

'There was a time,' said Bognor, 'when cooks were just cooks, and chefs worked at a handful of great hotels.'

'Or were French.'

'Quite.' Bognor watched the bead in his glass, saw the bubbles ascend and vanish as they broke the surface.

'Don't like him,' said Bognor.

'Doesn't make him a murderer.'

'Don't like his food either.'

'Nor does that.'

'I suppose not.'

They stared morosely at the dead flat-screen.

'So, you eliminate him from your enquiries?'

'I'll talk to a sous-chef or two just to firm up his alibi,

but basically he's eliminated, yes. Strange interviewing him. I felt like that greengrocer on *Celebrity Masterchef*. Nothing but meaningless superlatives and droolings about how he's getting a sense of well-rounded peach fragrance. I've never had snail porridge, but I'm more interested in discussing that, than I am in establishing his alibi. If you know what I mean.'

'Up to a point,' agreed Monica, 'though if he didn't have an alibi and was a murderer, that would make him interesting, wouldn't you say?'

Bognor considered this.

'You mean,' he said, 'that haute cuisine is more interesting than murder.'

'The other way round, actually. But the one against the other.'

'Hmm,' said Bognor, 'we live in a world which rates them both pretty high. After all, cooks and murderers make flawless celebrities, along with models and failed spin bowlers.'

'Especially if they can dance.'

They both laughed. Their world seemed real enough to them and yet, to dancing cooks and models, it would have carried just the whiff of make-believe that they ascribed to television, soundbites and the meretricious in general. You paid your money and you took your choice, and the future would deliver a verdict which would change according to the times, and whether or not the world survived. In the meantime, Bognor reckoned that all you could do was the best possible according to one's own lights, and not to be seduced by bright lights, instant success and a certain sort of suit.

Talking of which, he supposed that he really ought to interview Sir Branwell and Lady Fludd. In the event of things going wrong and of publicity ensuing, a failure to interview the Fludds would be held against him. Apocrypha College would be called in evidence to prove some sort of old school tie, and the fact that he and Monica were staying as guests up at the Manor would not look good. The headlines would scream, pseudo-egalitarians would snigger, and there would be a general consensus that it served him right, that he had fallen down on the job, and what could one expect from old-fashioned, fuddy-duddy, grumpy, long-lunching plutocrats anyway.

Bognor felt none of these things, and regarded himself as being, in practically every important aspect, at the well-honed cutting edge of life in general. Even so, he had seen enough of real life to know that he should appear to play by the book, if only to avoid having it thrown at him if things went wrong.

Which meant interviewing Branwell and Camilla, if only for form's sake.

It would yield nothing, but it would look good on paper and better still in the paper, if it ever got that far. The Fludds would dislike the interview, but the possible alternative was almost too dire to contemplate.

ELEVEN

Sir Branwell had never, well hardly ever, heard of anything so ludicrous in his life. It took the absolute chocolate digestive. It was the Bath Oliver to end all Bath Olivers. A real Huntley and Palmer. I mean he had never been so . . . well if the suggestion had come from anyone but Simon he would . . . on the other hand . . . was he absolutely certain . . . even in this day and age . . . I mean really.

And so on.

Bognor explained that the conversation was an essential formality. A formality, but essential nonetheless. It was simply a matter of insuring against criticism, of demonstrating efficiency, even-handedness and, above all, justifying the apparently high-handed decision to bypass the usual channels and allow Bognor to conduct the investigation instead of the local police force.

Simon began, naturally, by asking the same question with which he had opened his interview with the cook. Where had the Fludds been between roughly five and seven the previous day, that being the time, as near as could be ascertained, at which the Reverend Sebastian had passed by on to the other side?

'Oh for God's sake, you know perfectly well where we both were,' exploded Sir Branwell. 'We were here, with you. All the time, until Dorcas came in and told us that she had found her husband dead in church. You know that perfectly well.'

'That's not the point,' explained his interlocutor patiently. 'I know perfectly well, but the coroner won't, the court won't, the press won't. I need to have your alibi on the record so everyone can see it.'

'Bugger the record,' said the baronet. 'I have absolutely not the slightest interest in everyone, as you put it, seeing the record. I am entirely free to come and go as I please, without the world and his wife having to be told. It's completely outrageous. Where Camilla and I are, at any time of the day or night, is nobody's business but our own.'

'A man is dead,' said Bognor. 'Put yourself in everyone else's position.'

'On a point of fact,' Sir Branwell was being dangerously cool, 'a man is not dead. The Reverend Sebastian Fludd is dead. He was not a man in the accepted sense. He was the vicar of St Teath's and my cousin. I will not have his memory blasphemed in this fashion. "A man", indeed. That gives entirely the wrong impression. And I see absolutely no reason at all why I should put myself in everyone else's position. That is not where I want to be, and it is, to use your own word, completely "inappropriate". My position is my position, and I have no desire to be anywhere else. Nor is any useful purpose being served by pretending otherwise.'

'For my sake,' pleaded Monica. 'It'll make life easier for all of us. Help to beat off jawnalists. Allay criticism. Please.'

'I don't see it, Monica,' said Camilla, 'I really don't. We know where we were. You know where we were. Why should anyone else know?'

'That's the way it is,' said Bognor.

'Well, it shouldn't be,' said Sir Branwell snippily. 'Just because you say that's the way it is, doesn't mean that it's right and, or, proper. If people such as us don't stand up and allow ourselves to be counted, then what the hell's the point.'

'That's exactly what I'm asking,' said Bognor, trying to keep the triumph out of his voice. 'I just want you to stand up and be counted.'

'Don't be so childish,' said Sir Branwell, sounding childish. 'I decide whether or not we're going to stand up and be counted. Not any old Tom, Dick or Harry.'

'But,' said Monica, 'it's not any old Tom, Dick or Harry. It's Simon. Your old friend. Simon.'

'Simon,' said Sir Branwell, with an element of truth, 'is

acting on behalf of Tom, Dick and Harry. He doesn't fool me.'

'I'm going to write down that you and Camilla were with us in the Manor all through the time concerned,' said Bognor, 'and Monica and I will, if asked, swear to it.'

'Write what you like,' said Sir Branwell, adding surprisingly, 'Next question.'

'I wanted to ask about Sebastian. How well you knew him? What you thought made him tick. That sort of thing. Nothing specific. I just want to build up a picture.'

'That's more like it,' said the squire. 'Wouldn't want poor little Sebastian to become a cipher. Just because he's dead, doesn't make him a stiff. Rum bloke, very, but not without his points. And he was a Fludd. Never forget that. Quite a distant Fludd. Not part of the mainstream, but a Fludd all the same.'

'More like a puddle,' ventured Monica. 'I always thought of him as pretty wet but small scale.'

Sir Branwell ignored her. He regarded the sally as in poor taste and, in any case, Monica was a girl, a woman. All right for certain things: sex, flower arranging, cooking maybe, but not for opinions or thought or anything practical. For that, you needed a chap. Women were all very well in their way, indeed, you could say they helped make the world go round, but they were definitely only second fiddles. The orchestra was conducted and led by chaps, and the music was composed by one. God was a man, probably elderly, white-bearded, Anglo-Saxon. Almost certainly wore an Apocrypha tie and liked a drink on a cold day. He digressed. One did. And you couldn't quite say that the Reverend Sebastian was one of us, despite being a Fludd.

'What sort of Fludd was he exactly?' asked Bognor. He could see that family sensitivities were at work alongside the male chauvinism. It would be better not to offend them. If the family escutcheon were to be impugned, it would come better from one of themselves. Or not at all. Bognor knew enough about family nature to understand that, if rude things were to be said about the family, they would have to be said by a Fludd.

'Some sort of a cousin,' said Sir Branwell airily. 'There's a family tree thingy in the study and I think he features on that.'

'Descended from Flanagan?'

'Everyone was descended from Flanagan on one side or other of the proverbial blanket. Randy old goat.'

'He had the baronetcy?' asked Bognor, really not knowing.

'Briefly,' said Sir Branwell. 'He was number ten, but not for long. He inherited from some cousin.'

Life in the Fludd family was one cousin after another, reflected Bognor. This was not uncommon in titled families. The title itself zigzagged around, leaping from one branch to another. Chaps changed names from time to time in order to inherit the title, which was no more direct than the crown of England. The Fludds had been the equivalent of Plantaganets, Yorkists, Lancastrians, Tudors, Hanoverians, Schleswig-Holsteiners or whatever, ersatz Windsors and sundry assorted Krauts, Russians, New Zealanders, commoners, Normans, Anglo-Saxons and lesser breeds. Being baronets, however, they had an inordinately high opinion of themselves and took considerable pride in their Britishness, which was more imaginary than real.

Sir Flanagan was the only Fludd, however, who really merited even a footnote in the rich tapestry of English history. Not that the Fludds hadn't been all very well, in their way, ever since Athelstan Fludd had become an improbable friend of the Conqueror and been rewarded with the first of the fourteen titles. Fourteen was not that many, given the length of time Fludds had been around and the relatively scant time Fludds such as Flanagan had held the title. One or two of them had inherited when very young and lived to a very ripe old Fludd. One Fludd, a mediaeval Henry, was thought to have lived to be more than a hundred after acquiring the title before puberty. This compensated for the Montague Fludd who had been killed on the Somme. There were others, some of whom had not even inherited. An elder son had gone down with the White Ship and another perished at Trafalgar while serving as a midshipman on the Victory. No Fludd, however, had ever been Prime Minister, Chancellor or even Master of the family college. Their way was modest, local and unobtrusive. They were the salt of the earth, good men who did good things, but seldom remarkable.

'I think Sebastian was something to do with your great-aunt Mildred.' This was from Camilla, who had been uncharacteristically silent.

'We tend not to talk about Great Auntie Em,' said Sir Branwell, looking embarrassed. 'She was a bit of a black sheep. Friend of the Pankhursts; bookish. Swanned around on the fringe of the Bloomsbury business. Crossed swords with Lady Ottoline Morell over some chap. Said she even went abroad to have his child.'

'Great Aunt Mildred sounds rather fun,' said Monica, with feeling.

'Always thought to be something of a goer,' said the squire. 'Kept a boarding house somewhere near Biarritz, I believe. Played pétanque. Read Proust in the original. Before her time, unfortunately. Before anyone's time, if you ask me. I think Sebastian was something to do with her.'

'What exactly?'

'Haven't the foggiest. Great-aunt Em was married to Philip, who sounds a bit simple. Supposed to have had one or two sprogs with him, but I don't know that any were actually Philip's. If they were, then I suspect poor old Sebastian came down that line somehow. But I honestly don't know. He was a Fludd, all right. He had the Fludd ears. But I couldn't honestly say how exactly he fitted in.'

'Maybe he didn't,' said Bognor archly.

There was a conceit that people such as Sir Branwell didn't exist, that no one nowadays spoke like this, nor held such old-fashioned beliefs or maintained such old-fashioned values. They did, however. They were not celebrities and they tended to remain in the shires – or, as trendy people liked to believe, the sticks. They still wore their grandfather's three-piece suits, changed for dinner and sometimes boasted fob watches. They would outlive many flashier success stories, for these came and went like moths in the night, garish flutterbies who glowed briefly before fading away into crepuscular obscurity. The Fludds seldom troubled the tabloids, but they often seemed to stretch out for ever, gathering dust, but little or no moss.

'Oh, I was fond of Sebastian in his way,' said Branwell. 'He was family after all. Funny way of showing it, but we Fludds stick together, no matter what.'

'But there was a "matter what", if you see what I mean. A sense in which Sebastian wasn't one of you, despite being a Fludd, albeit from a cadet branch. How would you describe that?'

Sir Branwell gave the matter his attention.

'Bit of a lefty,' he said eventually. 'Not exactly a Bolshevik but pretty socialist. Read novels, which isn't exactly our bag. The sort of stuff which gets on the shortlist for prizes. I like Trollope. Now that's what I call writing. Sebastian liked foreign muck. Marques. That Peruvian chap. Llhosa. Girl's stuff. Not that I ever held it against him. In fact, we used to have quite animated conversations about books and that sort of thing.'

Bognor could believe it. Sir Branwell might do his best to appear stupid, but he didn't fool the Bognors.

'Would you say he had doubts?' he asked.

'Doubts?' echoed the squire. 'Doubts.' He rolled the world around as if it were some sort of cigar, or a recalcitrant piece of food that had got stuck in his teeth. More than an abstract idea. 'Sebastian wasn't into certainty,' he said eventually, 'which I found rather attractive. So many clerics are a pain in the bum; try to convert you to their way of thinking. Sebastian wasn't like that. I never heard him giving a lecture. Even his sermons asked questions, rather than provide answers. I liked that. Reassuring, very.'

'You don't think that this indecisiveness had anything to do with his death?'

Not for the first time Sir Branwell appeared to give the question some thought. Eventually, he said, 'Rum notion.' Then he thought some more and said, 'I suppose not being certain might have helped suicide, but, as it happens, I don't think he killed himself. Difficult to tie the knot and Sebastian wasn't practically inclined. Not one of nature's knot-tiers.

And, if someone else killed him, the doubt would be neither here nor there. But none of this matters a jot, because it won't bring him back. Which is why, basically, I think the whole investigation is a waste of time.'

TWELVE

'**B**ranwell and Camilla didn't do it,' said Bognor. 'I knew that already, but I needed to get it down in black and white. Besides which, I thought what he had to say about Sebastian was quite interesting.'

'Quite,' said Monica. She was easily bored, only interested in the really interesting; difficult to please.

They were sitting quietly in a corner of the maize. This was a modern number designed at Sir Branwell's request, and conceived and executed by Michael Ayrton. It was made of well-topiaried beech and was a tribute to the squire's unexpected complexity. The bench they sat on was of burnished something or other. Wood. No plaque. Sturdy. Modern. Designed to last.

'Well, I thought it was interesting. It can't be easy being Branwell.'

'Don't be ridiculous, darling,' she said. 'Nothing could be easier. He has a title, money, a nice house, reputation, and he's never done a hand's turn in his life.'

'That's not fair,' he expostulated.

'Maybe not,' she said, 'but who said anything about "fairness"? To echo the immortal words of Malcolm Fraser: "Life's not supposed to be fair."'

Malcolm Fraser was a tall, notably patrician, Australian prime minister who had many inherited acres of prime land, was born with silver spoons in every aperture and pretended that he had worked hard to get where he was. Monica evidently believed that Sir Branwell Fludd shared some of these attributes.

'I wouldn't want a literary festival named after me.'

'It's not named after Branwell,' protested Monica. 'It's named after Flanagan. Flanagan was an ancestor. Or not, as the case may be. I don't actually think he was a real ancestor. He didn't have the family ears.'

'It's called the Fludd Festival. Most people don't have a clue about Flanagan or who he was. They think it's named after Branwell. He's damned either way. Either he supports it, or he doesn't. It wasn't his idea.'

'Only because he's too lazy and uninspired. Branwell's never had an idea in his life and he's certainly never acted on one.' Monica was on a high horse. She often was. It suited her and she enjoyed being there, even if the position wasn't always logical.

'That's not fair.'

'Back to Malcolm Fraser,' she said. 'I'm extremely fond of Branwell and Camilla, but that doesn't mean that I approve of them. I think they're an affront, actually, and the literary festival is the most obvious source of irritation. It's not, as you put it, fair, and I think he's living off his ancestor's talent. I don't really object, except when I stop and think about it. But don't give me that ridiculous line about being him not being easy. Being the fourteenth baronet with your own literary festival is an extremely soft option.'

'I disagree,' he said. 'It was the council's idea, and if he supported it he was damned, just as he would have been damned if he had opposed it. They just wanted to extend the holiday season, and the Fludd name was a good way of doing it. They're the ones who are exploiting it. It wasn't Branwell's idea to call Mallborne the centre of Fludd Country and put up signs to prove it. In fact, he finds it pretty embarrassing.'

'Then, why not say so? He goes along with the idea and the money rolls in, while he wrings his hands in a weedy way and pretends to thinks it's all a bit vulgar and common.'

'On the contrary,' said Bognor, defending his old friend and fellow Apocrypha man, 'a lot of people think he's vulgar and common, and there's absolutely nothing he can do about it. Imagine the outcry if there was a story along the lines of "Fludd scion attacks family festival".'

'I disagree,' she said.

'Why? How? It's no use disagreeing for the hell of it; you have to have a reason.'

Their voices were ever so slightly raised, though they

were enjoying an argument, not having a domestic tiff. It was argument such as this that kept them going: adversarial, but not mortally so. Theirs was a learning process, not just because their verbal battles ended in an increased knowledge of the matter under debate, but because they always knew each other even better when they had finished. It was this mutual knowledge, honed over years of matrimonial bickering, that made them such a formidable team, both professionally and over the dinner table, and during the long weekend. It didn't pay to mess with the Bognors.

'He gets to seem to ride shotgun,' she said, 'but actually he's just riding on coat-tails. Other buggers' efforts. Like I said, he's never done a hand's turn, but he has this reputation. Everything's inherited; the festival most of all.'

It didn't seem like that to Bognor, though he had to admit that most things to do with Branwell Fludd were the result of what other people had achieved and what other people had left him. What Monica didn't seem to take into account was that the inheritance carried obligations, as well as benefits. Branwell was not his own person; he was determined by circumstance; his freedom of action was circumscribed. His prison might have gold bars, but it was still a cell.

'Branwell can't do what he wants,' he said, 'and that's limiting. He controls a living and that's a perk. But then a relation takes holy orders and comes to him as a supplicant. The church is in his gift, but he has to bestow it in a particular way to a particular person. That's an obligation.'

'*Noblesse oblige*,' she said.

He nodded. 'You could put it like that,' he agreed. 'It wouldn't be original, but, otherwise, it's about right.'

'Nice sort of obligation,' she said.

He smiled. This was an argument, he felt, that he had won.

'The point I am making,' he said, 'is that most of us are free to live our lives as we wish. In my case, I became a special investigator. No one asked me to become such a thing, but that's what I do. By the same token, I met and married you. The lack of children I suppose I regret, but that is outside our control, as are a number of other facts, such as our appearance, our life expectancy and so on. For

Branwell, it's different. Inheriting his title and Mallborne
Manor is limiting, but being descended from Flanagan
Fludd, and then having Councillor Smallwood of the
Mallborne District Council deciding to create a literary
festival with him as the central figure, creates further
constraints. I'm not saying that Branwell is not in a number
of portent respects a lucky and privileged bleeder, but he
can't lead his own life in his own way, like the way the rest
of us can.'

'Oh, all right,' said Monica with something approaching
grace. 'You win. What about Sebastian?'

'What about Sebastian?' This sounded like round two:
seconds out of the ring, ding-ding, start boxing.

'Would you say he had freedom to do as he wished? Or
was he circumscribed in the same way as Branwell?'

'Not in the same way as Branwell, no. On the whole, he
had complete freedom of choice to begin with, but then the
minute he got religion in a serious professional way he was
hamstrung. So are the rest of us, but becoming a reverend
imposes a tighter straitjacket than the one most of us are
laced into. The fact that he did it himself doesn't make it
any easier. Rather the reverse.'

'OK,' she said, returning to her *moutons*. 'So did he jump?
Or was he pushed?

And, in the end, does it make a blind bit of difference.
Is, in other words, any useful purpose established by establishing exactly what happened. Wouldn't we be better off,
as Branwell appears to be suggesting, in simply drawing a
line under the messy business and moving on. Nothing we
can do will bring him back. Branwell's right there.'

'Don't think I hadn't thought of it,' agreed Bognor. A
dove cooed from nearby. The Fludds owned a mediaeval
dovecote and had a flock of white birds to match. They
made a mess and a soft plangent sound which was agreeably soothing. Time was when there would have been more
and would have supplemented the larder. Today, they were
ornamental only. 'There's a lot to be said for letting events
take their natural course. The trouble is that my whole *raison
d'etre* is predicated on not doing so.'

'You said it,' she said with feeling.

'Branwell would let his cousin rest in peace,' said Bognor.

'For all the wrong reasons.'

'He believes in letting things follow their natural course. Assume their own shape in their own way. Ride the waves. Maybe he's right. In any case, who are we to say which reasons are right? There's more than one way of playing God.'

'If Sebastian had died of natural causes, then maybe so. But if he didn't . . .'

'We know he didn't die of natural causes,' said Bognor. 'He was strung up. Hanged from the rafters of his own church.'

'You know what I mean,' she protested. 'If he killed himself, then there's an even better reason for leaving it all alone. If no one else is involved, then no one else is involved. We have no right to strike attitudes. If he was killed against his wishes, then that's a different matter.'

'There was no sign of a struggle,' he said.

'We have to wait for the pathologist's report. That will tell us for certain. But I agree. On the face of it, there's no sign of a struggle, but that doesn't mean he wasn't killed against his wishes. He could have been frightened by a man with a knife who forced him to make it look like suicide by hanging; then kicked the stool away when Sebastian wasn't expecting it. If it happened like that, then there wouldn't be signs of a struggle.'

'A lot of hypothesis; precious little evidence.'

'A lot of murders are like that,' she said. 'An awful lot are solved by a bluff that's so convincing the guilty party owns up. But the so-called evidence wouldn't stand up in court. Confession induced by bluff. That's why successful detectives are consummate poker players.'

'But I don't play poker.'

'Exactly. Case rests.' She laughed.

He lunged at her, but she was too quick, and stood, smoothing her skirt as she did so.

'The only real evidence is the hymns on the board.'

'Which may be a complete red herring,' he said. 'Had any more thoughts?'

'No. Afraid not.' She glanced at her watch. It was 6.15 p.m. 'And talking of church, which we sort of were, don't you think we'd better cut along if we're going to catch the festival service and your friend the bishop? I wonder, incidentally, if Sebastian had worked out what he was going to say. We haven't found any notes. He might have been going to confess. You know. Say something revelatory and incriminating, and then take poison, or plunge a dagger into himself in front of a full congregation. Now that would have been dramatic.'

Bognor stood and adjusted his tie. The garish stripes of Apocrypha College. He guessed Sir Branwell would be wearing the same. It had become a ritual.

'Poor taste,' he said. 'Vulgar gesture. Far-fetched suggestion.'

'If you can't make jokes about sudden death,' said Monica, 'I don't know what you can make jokes about.'

'I suppose not,' he said.

The bells of St Teath had started to ring, drowning out the sad cooing of the Fludds' doves. The congregation was heading towards the pews, as it did every year on the Sunday before the literary festival began. For the first time ever, the sermon would not be delivered by the Reverend Sebastian Fludd, nor would he take the service or say grace at the supper in The Fludd, aka the Two by Two, shortly afterwards.

His absence would be felt, however, and his sudden death would cast a pall over tonight's proceedings and much of what was scheduled for the week ahead.

'Your friend the Bish had better be good,' said Monica.

THIRTEEN

The church was packed.

It always was. Correction. It always was for this annual service preceding the Fludd Lit Fest. On the average Sunday, at Holy Communion, Matins or Evensong, attendance was sparse. Sir Branwell and Lady Fludd sat sadly in the family pew at one or other of these services, but otherwise the faithful were considerably less attentive and dutiful than even a few years earlier. The church was always full at Easter and Christmas, but apart from this, and the annual Festival service, it echoed in effective emptiness. The vicar, the choir and the organist turned up, and one or two hardy regulars, but that was all. The rest stayed away pursuing secular rites and rituals.

This was the way of the Church of England. Time was when it had been the Tory party at prayer, but now even the traditional Conservative Party was little more than a memory of blue rosettes, feudalism and soapbox oratory. Muslims, foreign sects, and even the Methodists and Roman Catholics, seemed to be gaining ground, or at least standing steady, but the lukewarm moderate established church was no longer part of the required procedure.

Tonight, however, the ancient building was full of Mallborne and its visitors. The ghost of the late Reverend hung heavily over the service and all the suspects were there. Sir Branwell and Lady Fludd had kept a couple of places for the Bognors, who dutifully squeezed into the box pew alongside them. Just behind them, though decently below the salt, were the butler, Harry Brandon, and his wife Peggoty. The widow Dorcas Fludd was snivelling appropriately in off-black weeds. Brigadier Blenkinsop and his wife Esther sung lustily in tweed and responded noisily in all the right places. Vicenza Book kept shtum, waiting presumably until she could command attention from centre stage, and Martin Allgood sat near the back of the building behind a pillar and observed beadily. Gunther Battenburg was not there; presumably preparing dinner in the Fludd kitchens.

All was as one would hope and expect, and as orderly as Sir Branwell would have wished.

The service itself was robust and conventional: middle of the road as only rural C of E could be on a high and holy day, and the whole affair made Bognor comfortable. He was surrounded by the sights and sounds of his growing-up and he drew strength from their permanence.

The Saxon church was full of English spring flowers of a kind he associated with cottage gardens, rather than municipal beds. The sweet peas smelt, the wild garlic and valerian were classified as weeds elsewhere, but here they were encouraged to rampage over the pulpit, lectern and font. All was amateur, in a friendly way, unless you scratched the smiling surface and revealed the steely professionalism beneath. Iron fist in velvet glove. The congregation was led by the choir in 'All Things Bright and Beautiful', 'Fight the Good Fight' and the 23rd psalm. The readings were from the King James Bible, the Authorized Version, the only decent committee job known to man.

The bishop was the senior cleric present by a mile. A couple of lay readers from the neighbourhood were offici-ating, standing in for the Reverend Sebastian, and hating each other in a decidedly unchristian way, if the Bognors' sixth sense was to be trusted. It was difficult to upstage one another during a church stage, but it seemed to the Bognors that these two did their best, though even this rivalry was strangely reassuring, for it reminded Bognor of the chaplains at school – technically equals, but for ever, it seemed to him and his friends, competing for supremacy. Or at least the appearance of supremacy.

Finally, the bishop's turn came. He, more than anyone, cut a figure that was at once friendly and familiar, but also contrived to be scary. On the one hand, he was benign, short and fat, on the other, his cope, mitre and crook made him seem forbidding and frightening. His smile was beatific, but his frown was full of the wrath of God. He was, after all,

God's representative in Lymington and the surrounding diocese. When he smiled, the lilies of the field smiled back, but when he looked cross, the ground trembled. Yea, verily, he was Bishop Ebenezer and it would be sensible to keep the right side of him.

From the pulpit, he began by presenting his right side as if to the manor born by quoting a Biblical text in the traditional manner. 'My text tonight is taken from the Gospel according to Saint John, beginning at the first verse of the first chapter: "In the beginning was the word and the word was with God and the Word was God."' And then he paused and looked down and around at the congregation, seemingly undecided about whether to telegraph the smile of God or the frown of God, but, instead, merely repeating the words in an incantatory manner: '"In the beginning was the word and the word was with God and the Word was God."'

Once more, he looked round the congregation, seemingly uncertain whether to smile or frown, whether to play God the merciful or the God of wrath. In the end, he seemed to hold both in check and play God the neutral: a sort of 'don't know' in one of Miles Kington's plenary sessions.

'Of course, we all know that the word "word" is a translation of the Greek "logos" and is open to any one of a number of different interpretations. I won't, however, insult your intelligence by going down that route. Apart from anything else, I feel it would be something of a cop-out. The authors of that majestic book wrote "word" and I feel we owe it to them to believe that they meant what they wrote, and that therefore they believed in the supremacy of the word. For them the word is the word of God and the word of God reigns supreme.'

He was a long way off insulting their collective intelligence, let alone copping out. The Brigadier had certainly never come across 'logos'. Nor Vicenza Book. Martin Allgood, well, yes, up to a point and in a manner of speaking. The Bognors, certainly. Branwell Fludd, perhaps surprisingly, yes. His wife, no.

In a curious way, it was an episcopal sorting of goats from sheep, men from boys, cognoscenti from buffoons.

'How appropriate, therefore, that we should be meeting at the beginning of this tenth literary festival in the House of God; a God who, according to the Holy Gospel, not only believed in the word, but believed in the word above all else. All this week, we celebrate the word in its various shapes and patterns and glories. Tonight, however, we celebrate God's word in God's house.

'And what, I ask myself, as we all must, at this beginning of a week of celebration of God's unique gift, what exactly was God's message? To what use did he put that wonderful word which he gave us, and which St John tells us about so memorably and so beautifully? What exactly did God mean? What exactly did God say? His is, by any standard, the greatest book in the world, and yet what precisely is its message? What exactly does it say? What is the message which echoes so vibrantly throughout its pages?'

Bishop Ebb was beginning to lose the attention of even those listeners who had been paying some attention, and not just listening to the more or less acceptable noise that he made. He spoke in a passably well-modulated middle-church way, some way short of the wonderfully nasal C of E fashion adopted by Alan Bennett for his seminally parodic sermon ('My Brother Esau is an hairy man but I . . .') in *Beyond the Fringe*, but also divorced from what generally passed for received speech in the early years of the twentieth century. The bishop spoke prose from the pulpit in an appropriate manner. It would have passed muster on the BBC's 'Thought for the Day', alongside the breezy Balliolity of the Reverend Lionel Blue, the people's Rabbi. As a matter of fact, Bishop Ebb had appeared on 'Thought for the Day' and was considered by the powers that be at the corporation to be rather better than such performers as Chartres, the Bishop of London (too Old Testament prophet) and Harris, the former Bishop of Oxford (too serpentine, sibilant and reminiscent of Caiaphas, the High Priest). Ebenezer Lariat fell well short of being trendy, but he was nearer the common man who listened to the radio than any of his counterparts.

Today's bishop moved on to Flanagan Fludd. He had

obviously googled Flanagan Fludd and was forced, therefore, to rely heavily on the Wikipedia entry which had been
composed by Sir Branwell and Lady Fludd with a little help
from the Bognors some years ago. It had been 'improved',
as is the way with Wikipedia entries, that is to say it now
contained even more 'information' whose factual basis was
questionable. This meant that the bishop's stuff on the eponymous festival centrepiece was thin and slightly doubtful.

This, in turn, meant that the Fludds and the Bognors
switched off for the stuff about the Mallborne Pageants of
the 1890s, for the collaboration with Louis Napoleon Parker
and the famous rhyming version of King Lear. He vaguely
heard that Flanagan might perhaps not have been a man of
God in the strictly conventional sense, but that he was assur-
edly a man of His Word, and therefore blessed in some
indefinable but definite fashion, and that he was generally
speaking a Good Thing, in the Sellar and Yeatman sense.
Actually, it was the festival and the present generation of
Fludds that were his most significant and lasting bequest,
and none the worse for that.

The bishop padded out his sentences on Flanagan Fludd
with references to Tennyson (whom Fludd had once met)
and the optimism of Locksley Hall ('Let the great world
spin for ever down the ringing grooves of change'), despite
no evidence that Fludd had ever read the epic verses, nor
indeed anything much, except for his own outpourings,
which were, if truth be told, more reminiscent of William
McGonegall than of the poet Tennyson, but let it pass;
Flanagan was one of the great impresarios, a *flâneur* and,
above all, a man of His Word.

Here, the bishop paused and looked around the church
with that curious mixture of threat and mateyness, before
coming out with words which made the inhabitants of the
family pew suddenly sit bolt upright.

'Above all,' he intoned, 'Flanagan was a Fludd.'

He beamed again. Beatific yet baleful. It was not a smile
in the usual sense, but more the sort of rictus grimace with
which one brought really bad tidings. It was a more in
sorrow than in anger sort of movement. He was telling his

listeners that this was going to hurt him more than them. He was also signalling that this was not true, but necessary public relations. Bognor had spent years of his upbringing listening to teachers such as this. They said one thing, while meaning something quite different. What they said was nice, what they meant was nasty. Life was full of people like that. Even Bishops. Even Bishops who, on the whole, one rather liked.

'Fludds,' said Bishop Ebb, 'may come, and Fludds may go. Unlike our Lord, none go on for ever.'

He smiled again, for what he had just said represented the nearest a bishop in a pulpit came to a joke.

'Most Fludds, like the rest of us, have but a short time to live. Many manage their allotted three score years and ten. Some manage more and some less, but it matters not a lot, for the Lord giveth and the Lord taketh away, and he has an unpleasant habit of giving life on the one hand, while removing it on the other. It is no coincidence that the two most significant dates on the Christian calendar come at Christmas and at Easter. These represent, first, the giving of life and, second, the taking away of that same gift. Life is a gift of God, but so too is death.

'No one here will be unaware of the fact that our Lord has stretched out his hand and taken away a Fludd from amongst us. "Come in, Sebastian," he said, only yesterday in this very place. "Come in, Sebastian. For your time is up."

The bishop looked round the silent killing ground, obviously satisfied at the way in which his words seemed to have grabbed the attention of all those present, and he repeated, softly and slowly:

'Come in, Sebastian . . . Your time is up!'

FOURTEEN

Bognor had never previously thought of the Lord His God as a fairground attendant, nor as the man in charge of pleasure boats on an artificial lake. He was, however, open to new thoughts, and this one pleased him. He rolled it around his mind as if it were a toy that he had just unwrapped. He tasted it, as if it were an interesting wine to savour, or the first in a packet of Tim Tams or Cherry Ripes; an opportunity to decide once and for all whether Marmite was better than Vegemite. He considered Sebastian a Vegemite sort of priest – bland, all-things-to-all-men, not spikey and sharp like Marmite. He liked people to be Marmites. Difficult presences. The Reverend Sebastian had been a Vegemite in life, bearing the imprint of the last person to whom he had spoken. A true Marmite would have resisted and been a constantly awkward customer. It was only in death that Sebastian had become a Marmite.

'Life,' said the bishop, 'goes on. Like the show. And my friend – our friend – Sebastian, would have wished it that way.'

Only a bishop, thought Simon. Having a pulpit enabled you to look down on other people, wearing ornate frocks and a purple vest gave you a spurious authority, a mitre raised your height and a crook was a staff to lean on, as well as a club with which to beat. If he, or any of his bêtes noires in government or public, had dared to utter such clichés, they would have been laughed at and scorned. A bishop, however, could get away with such banality.

'There are two lives here,' he said from the pulpit, with all the authority of his vestments and his position. 'The life temporal, fleeting and, perhaps even as the political theorist Thomas Hobbes would have us believe, "nasty, brutish, solitary and short". And the life everlasting, which is a thing of beauty beyond our comprehension, for eternity is a concept we cannot comprehend.

'Our friend, my friend, Sebastian, has departed the first of these lives. He has done so unexpectedly and, to our conventional way of thinking, before his time. The reason for, and the manner of his departure, have to be ascertained, for that is the law of this land in which we live. We are singularly fortunate in that we have in our midst one whose whole life has been concerned with such sudden unexpected comings and goings. I have known him for what passes on this Earth for quite a long time, even if, in the eyes of the Almighty, it is no more than a blinking of an eye. I am confident that our friend, my friend, Simon, will solve the matter of Sebastian's sudden departure correctly, according to the laws of this our land, and that he will do so decorously, respectfully and without fuss.'

Once again, he paused in a manner which Simon was beginning to find suspiciously theatrical. Ebenezer was too like a stage bishop – an episcopal Robertson Hare, an ecclesiastical Derek Nimmo. Too much to be quite true. If he had not known that he was real, Bognor would have had his suspicions. He was like a man playing at being a bishop, a layman assuming a disguise.

'I,' said the Rt Rev. Ebenezer, 'have no more standing in this world than any of you. We are all equal in the sight of the law, and it is in the sight of the law that justice will be done and will be seen to be done. I trust implicitly in my friend Sir Simon Bognor, and I trust that you too will echo that trust and bring that which passes for guilty to be brought to that which passes for justice. I yield to no man in my respect for the true course of such temporal affairs, and yet I feel obliged to enter an eternal caveat.'

He looked around and smiled, though this time it was more of a snarl than a smile.

'But,' he said, 'and it is an important, an all important "but", there is another country, another judge, another justice. And in the world where this is so, I have a certain locus. I repeat: I have no more status than any of you when it comes to the law of the land, which I respect. However, in the law of God, the eternal, the everlasting, the law to end all laws, I do have a certain standing, for I stand before you as a man of God, as His representative on this Earth, which is of his making. His motive in doing so passeth all understanding and his ways are not the ways of mere mortals. And by the same token his justice is not the same as mortal justice, nor his giving, nor his taking away.'

No pause here, even though the technical construction of his sermon might have demanded it. The bishop was beginning to believe in his own rhetoric; his material was getting the better of him.

'In other words, Sir Simon will do his duty and we must assist him in whatever way we can. But there is a higher judge, a higher justice, a higher truth. The one does not invalidate the other, nor does it mean that we must stand in the way of man's law and our own puny attempts to serve it. It does mean, however, that we can not pretend to an understanding of Almighty God, his infinite mercy and his absolute love. God has the final word, for as the evangelist has it, He is not only with the word, he is the word itself, the first word as well as the last.

'I cannot pretend,' and here he lowered his voice like the old ham he was, 'to know the workings of the divine mind. None of us can, but rest assured. His is the Might and His the Right.'

The Bognors exchanged glances and raised all four eyebrows.

Bognor himself was unsure about this division between the temporal and the divine. It seemed to him that the law of the land was running a rather dismal second to the Law of God, which put him into a subsidiary position behind the Lord and his vicar on Earth, viz Ebenezer Lariat. The bishop would say that though, and he had the advantage of the pulpit and an awe-inspiring frock. Bognor reckoned that he too would cut an authoritative figure in episcopal gear, especially when speaking from on high, with a strict ban on heckling or vocal dissent of any kind. Whoever heard of a bishop being disagreed with publicly – especially in church.

On the other hand, his was a strong hand and he had the

endorsement of God's representative. True, this support only extended as far as this life and not the one hereafter, in which, in any case, he was not sure he believed. Who needed authority to deal with heaven, hell and purgatory when he and a majority of ordinary people, including those gathered in St Teath's did not even believe? No point in one's writ running in a fictitious place which didn't exist. Better the nitty gritty, the here and now, than an illusory life to come. In any case, the bishop would say that, wouldn't he? No, on balance, he was quite pleased.

'Already,' continued His Grace, 'there are rumours surrounding the sudden and unexpected passing of the late Sebastian. It is part of my function as his friend and as God's appointed representative for this diocese to put an end to such rumours as quickly and as definitively as possible. I have already heard it said that the Reverend Sebastian was gay, I have already heard it said that the Reverend Sebastian was in financial difficulties, involving not just the church roof but some of our most notorious bankers.' Here he smiled again, for he had made another approximation to a joke. 'I have even heard that the Reverend Sebastian's relationship with his bosses, both here and now, as it were, were not what they were.

'Let me say,' and here the bishop drew himself up to his full height, which though an inconsiderable five foot four in bare feet, was pretty intimidating when aided by the pulpit and the mitre, 'once and for all, that those rumours are poppycock, balderdash and completely inappropriate. Not only are they false rumours, but the expression of any seditious thoughts regarding our late brother, nay father, in Christ are, *ipso facto*, bad, evil and naughty. It is bad to venture a false opinion, but it is even worse, in this instance, to venture an opinion at all. I ask, indeed, I command you, to keep any thoughts about the death of the Reverend Sebastian Fludd. I cannot, of course, prevent you from having thoughts. Nor can I prevent you from conveying such thoughts to Sir Simon, but as far as the Lord God Almighty is concerned, such thoughts should be kept to yourselves where they truly belong.'

The Bognors had been doing their best to follow what, for want of a better word, should be described as 'reason', even though both of them felt the bishop was short of logic, and that he was falling back on a position which even mild agnostics such as they believed to be dubious.

Even Bishop Ebb showed evidence of coming to an end of his sermon, if not his tether, for, quite suddenly, he snapped into a peroration. 'So,' he intoned, 'I have two messages. One is a message of warning, and that concerns the death of your pastor and his unexpected removal from this earth. The other concerns the Fludd Festival of Arts and Literature, and expresses the hope that you will enjoy the festival and that much good may come of it.

'And, in conclusion, I would tell you that both the warning and the hope are to be respected and obeyed, for as Saint John the Divine tells us at the very beginning of his gospel, "In the beginning was the Word and the word was with God and the Word was God".

'And now, in the name of God the Father, God the Son and God the Holy Ghost, Amen.'

So saying, he paused again, beamed at the congregation, made the sign of the cross and tripped majestically down the steps of the pulpit, as the two lay-readers managed to announce that the members of the congregation should rise and sing the hymn 'Bread of Heaven' to the tune of Cwm Rhondda. Number 296 in *Hymns Ancient and Modern*, the 1950 Revised Edition. 'Guide me, O thou Great Jehovah, pilgrim through this barren land.' This was the traditional offering at Welsh rugby internationals in Cardiff and on the eve of the Fludd Festival in St Teath's Church, Mallborne. As such, it was a signal that all was right with the world, and it was, as Sir Branwell had hoped, business as usual.

And yet, it wasn't.

Outside, on that crisp spring evening, as the churchgoers milled around the Great West Door of their place of worship, there was a buzz of speculation which the words of the Lord their God and of his representative in the diocese had been unable to quell.

'I always thought there was something odd . . .' was the beginning of one conversation.

'Say what you like, but . . .' was the beginning of another.

'So, who do you think did it?' was the question which began a third.

This was not at all what the bishop had hoped to achieve as he thundered forth from the pulpit. His voice was evidently no more than tinkling brass and his message lay forlorn and unheeded. It might as well never have been uttered for all the good that it had done, and the bishop, passing among his flock flapped his ears and was duly dismayed.

Eventually, he found Sir Simon and Lady Bognor conversing with their hosts Sir Branwell and Lady Fludd.

'Over to you, dear boy,' said the Rt Reverend Ebenezer Lariat, rubbing his hands with a display of enthusiasm which was more apparent than real. 'Over to you, dear boy!'

FIFTEEN

They weren't at all sure about the snail porridge, which was greyish and tasted of, well, porridge and snails. It was followed by baked haunch of emu with a mousseline of apricots, and hake cheek and sprouts à la Fludd; finished off by fudge fondue with grape nuts on a whitebait foam. Bognor thought the emu haunch was delicious, though he wasn't sure about the rest. Most people weren't sure about the emu either. Gastronomic certainty was a wonderful thing, and at least at the manor you knew where you were. Here, at the Two by Two, you could have been anywhere except where you actually were, which was middle England.

Before Gunther, the food at the Fludd Arms was more predictable and in a sad way perhaps more apt. This evening's was at the cutting edge, cooked by a chef at the acme of his profession. The fact that most of the diners thought it inedible was, frankly, neither here nor there. It would play well on TV and in the newspapers and magazines. It was the sort of scoff that would raise the Fludd Lit Fest in to the front rank, alongside Hay-on-Wye and Cheltenham.

This was the thinking of the public relations department at the *Daily Beast* who sponsored the festival, and whose literary editor would be arriving with selected 'jawnalists' some time to tomorrow. Sir Branwell drew the line at the *Beast* and its sponsorship; refused to have them in the house; hadn't realized that Gunther Battenburg was their idea until too late. Actually, considering that Gunther was some sort of kraut and produced disgusting, overpriced and pretentious food, the Fludds thought he was quite a good egg.

The Bognors were split up, but were at quite an important table. The tables were round and there were eight diners at each. The Bognors were with Brigadier and Mrs Blenkinsop, Vicenza Book and the bishop, and Martin Allgood and someone from his publishers who was described as his 'publicist', but who seemed to know little or nothing about books, whether by Allgood or anyone else, and whose high cheekbones, pert breasts and generally gamine appearance, suggested that she was his girlfriend and had no literary pretensions. Literary pretensions were, as far as Bognor could see, rather old hat as far as cutting edge festivals and publishers were concerned. Several times he had heard festival organizers and publishers say that their profession (always a profession never a job, nor a trade) would be quite agreeable, if it were not for authors. He had even heard TV producers debating how they could avoid actually having to read books before deciding whether they should be turned into some kind of visual treat. The bishop may have thought that the word was paramount and the Bible a best-seller, but this was a view not widely shared by those in the know, at the sharp end, who actually determined what the rest of the world – poor saps – actually read.

The point of the round tables was that none should be seen to be more important than others. It was a sort of Orwellian conceit, for it was perfectly obvious that, even if all tables were equal, some were more equal than others. The Bognors' was, happily, one such and, once the bishop had said grace (the usual Anglo-Saxon), those who had made it to tables obviously above the salt looked a little smug while sipping their elderflower cocktails, and those who found themselves just as obviously below, looked predictably sour.

'Jolly sound sermon, Your Grace,' said Brigadier Blenkinsop, leaning across the bowl of valerian and sweet peas which formed the centrepiece of each table. 'Just the ticket. First class.'

Ingratiating wanker, thought both Bognors, smiling at him.

The bishop looked slightly uncomfortable and asked if anyone had heard the latest test score.

Bognor said, truthfully, that the last he had heard, England were 125 for nine, although the last pair had put on more than thirty.

'Sounds about right,' said Ebenezer, who really was keen on the game, still an episcopal characteristic, though not a mandatory one. Time was when the country was full of cricketing clergy. Now, however, there were precious few clerics, and very few of them had either the time or the inclination for cricket. Not like the days of Prebendary Wickham of Martock, who kept bees and the Somerset wicket.

'Blenkinsop,' said the brigadier, shaking hands around the table. He and Bognor had met somewhere or other before. Bognor remembered, Blenkinsop didn't. Remembrance and amnesia were instructive; they said a lot about both people.

'Come here often?' he asked Monica, originally. She was on his right, which Blenkinsop obviously took as a compliment. Monica didn't.

'It depends what you mean by often?' she said, being deliberately difficult.

'So, you've been before?' Blenkinsop didn't notice. Or, if he did, he was determined not to show it.

'Yes,' agreed Monica, not bothering to come up with anything more ambiguous.

'May I ask why?' the brigadier asking anyway.

'My husband and Sir Branwell were at the same college together. At Oxford. They both read Modern History. Shared tutorials. That sort of thing.'

The brigadier had been to the Royal Military Academy at Sandhurst, which was not at all the same. He nodded, privately put out, publicly at ease, consummately so.

'Oxford, eh.'

'Yes.' Monica had been there too. She read Mods and Greats on a scholarship at Somerville, but judged it unwise to say so just now. It was where she had first met Simon, but she thought it better to keep quiet about that too.

'Mmmm,' said the brigadier, and turned speculatively to his left which was where Martin Allgood's girlfriend was sitting.

'How about you?' he asked, managing to appear raffish. 'Were you at Oxford too?'

On receiving the answer 'No, actually', Brigadier

Blenkinsop seemed to relax, and concentrated on his neighbour and her cleavage, which was more obvious than Monica's, even if its owner had not been to Oxford.

Monica's right-hand neighbour was Martin Allgood.

'I enjoyed *Rubbish*,' she told him, naming one of his best-known books. It had been shortlisted for the Booker.

'I hated it,' said Allgood, shovelling snail porridge into himself as if it were all that stood between himself and starvation. 'Pig to write. Cost me a relationship. Reputation has dogged me ever since. Still, I'm glad you enjoyed it.'

He smiled wolfishly, displaying two rows of all-too-perfect teeth.

'And are you enjoying Mallborne?'

'Beats work,' he said.

She winced. It was obviously going to be one of those evenings. All this and three-star Michelin food as well. She sighed.

Her husband, meanwhile, was seated between the brigadier's wife, Esther, and Vicenza Book. The brigadier's wife, mouth like a prune, sensible hair, sensible dress, sensible shoes, which he could not see but sensed nonetheless, oozed sense and sensibility, and looked like hard work. He decided to go for Vicenza Book who had a décolletage that made Allgood's girlfriend look scrawny, and a mouth and come-hither eyes that suggested more barmaid than world-class soprano. Though, reasoned Bognor, there was no reason not to be both.

'I gather you're singing tomorrow in the big tent?'

'Yup,' said Miss Book, her mouth full of emu and apricot. 'And you're the police. I don't like police.'

'In a manner of speaking,' he agreed. 'I'm investigating the death. But I'm doing it instead of the police. I don't like them either.'

'Good to hear it,' she said, swallowing hard. 'If that's an emu, my father's the pope. Just chicken tarted up, if you ask me. I sing as Vicenza Book, but my friends call me Dolly. Pleased to meet you, Si.'

And she stuck out a hand which Bognor shook with enthusiasm. He decided he liked Ms Book, aka Dolly.

'Hi, Dolly,' he said. 'I hope you don't mind?'

'Cool,' she said, which could have meant anything, but which Bognor took to mean assent.

'What exactly are you singing?' he asked politely, though he sensed that Dolly didn't do politeness.

'Usual load of crap,' she said. 'Plus a bit of Faure's requiem and what they're describing as a "medley" by Flanagan Fludd. That really is crap. Old man Fludd makes Andrew Lloyd Webber look original. Everything's like, you know, pastiche Gilbert and Sullivan. They say Queen Victoria liked to hum along to Fludd. Typical effing royalty. Ever done a Royal Variety Performance?'

Bognor said he hadn't had the pleasure.

'Then don't,' said Ms Book. 'Absolute crap. None of them are interested. Couldn't sing a note. Only one who could was that Princess Margaret. Liked a smoke and a drink. Dead, but she could tinkle the ivories. Or so they say. Mind you, she liked tinkling more than just ivories.' And she let out a mirthless cackle which would sound witchlike when she had grown into it. Bognor reckoned she had been at the booze, but could not think how as it was flowing like treacle. She either had a very low tolerance for alcohol or carried her own flask.

'Been here long?' he asked, eye on a possible alibi.

'Came down yesterday afternoon to have a look at the old place. Me Mum used to work here. Right here, when it was the Fludd Arms. Proper little knocking shop by all accounts. All sorts of people used to come down from London for dirty weekends. You'd never guess who. Royalty and all.'

'Probably better at that sort of thing than the other kind of Royal Variety.'

She laughed again. Immoderately. One or two people turned to look. The brigadier was one. He was obviously not enjoying himself and was half-inclined to share in the joke, except that he obviously suspected – correctly – that there was no real joke involved.

'Anyway,' she said, pulling herself together rapidly and giving him a queer look. 'I was here when the poor old

beggar snuffed it. I didn't know him. I can't really account
for my movements. And I didn't do it. Next question.'

Bognor couldn't think of one.

Instead, he bit into the white stuff on his side plate and
said, 'Is this bread?'

She bit into hers, made a face and said, 'Toilet paper
more like.'

For the rest of the meal, Bognor swapped inane pleas-
antries with the soprano, managing to virtually ignore Esther
Blenkinsop who suffered in silence, picked at her food, and
was just as ignored by Martin Allgood on her other side.
She didn't enjoy the meal any more than her husband, but
she made less effort to conceal the fact.

Ms Book on the other hand consumed her fudge fondue
with gusto, though she left her whitebait foam, which she
referred to as 'fish froth', a description which Bognor
preferred. In deference to his companion, he too left his
whitebait, while doing his best with the fudge, which he
thought as disgusting as most of the rest of the meal.

The only proper speech was a welcome from a tiny
Scottish person called William Glasgow, who rose from a
long way below the salt and who plainly did all the work.
He held the title of 'Festival Convenor'.

'To all those who do not actually live here but are here
as guests of the Fludd Festival, I say welcome,' he said.
'Welcome to Mallborne.'

The Fludds scowled. As far as they were concerned, they
were the only people entitled to issue a welcome, or otherwise. Mr Glasgow was an impostor. And a paid pipsqueak
to boot.

Glasgow's was a poor speech, but a welcome respite nonetheless. He got tied in knots over the late priest, got the
punchline at the wrong end of a story involving Scotsmen,
Irishmen, Welshmen and Englishmen, and neglected to
mention the brigadier who appeared unfazed, but whose wife
seemed furious. Nevertheless, it made a change, and the
Bognors enjoyed it for its amateurishness. There was too
much polish around, too much style getting in the way of
substance. Bit like life, actually.

When Mr Glasgow had finished, Bognor leant across to
the brigadier and said, 'I wonder if I might have a word
afterwards? In confidence. In private.'

'Of course,' said Brigadier Blenkinsop. 'Not a problem.
Delighted.'

His wife, Esther, who heard the invitation and its accept-
ance, and was obviously not included in either, pursed her
lips even more than before, and was clearly even less happy
than hitherto.

And it wasn't just the food or the company.

SIXTEEN

The brigadier's was a Highland Park, which he said he hadn't tasted since he was on manoeuvres in the Orkneys some twenty years ago. He remembered the battalion attending matins in St Magnus' Cathedral in Kirkwall. Very red. Rather gaunt. Mind you, he liked his churches austere. Like religion. No time for smells, bells and poncing about. Bognor's was a calvados. He paid. He usually did. In more ways than one.

'So what can I do for you?' The brigadier didn't beat about the bush. Brigadiers didn't. That was part of what being a brigadier was all about. Like short sentences. Staccato. Very.

'Cheers,' said the brigadier planting his bottom (ample) in an armchair (capacious, chintzy, leftover from the last regime) by the fire (roaring). 'I'm afraid I didn't know the reverend gentleman. But fire away. Ball's in your court. Cheers.' And he raided his glass and leant back in anticipation.

The first question was the usual one about where exactly the brigadier had been the previous day between five and seven. The answer was disarming and impossible. He had been in his room at the hotel doing *The Times* crossword with Esther. This was a habitual occupation and Bognor had no doubt that Mrs Blenkinsop would corroborate her husband. What's more, the two of them would certainly be able to provide a convincing account of the clues. The brigadier said they had completed the puzzle in an hour and ten minutes, which was about usual. They almost always completed it, and they usually took between an hour and an hour and twenty minutes. He was probably telling the truth, thought Bognor, but the alibi wouldn't hold water in a court of law. Few alibis did. Not many people knew what they were doing from one moment to the next, even when they were doing it. If you saw what he meant.

'You know, that's not really a cast-iron alibi?' he asked.

The brigadier shifted his bottom and shrugged.

'Best I can do,' he said. 'Reception will confirm that they didn't have a key. They saw both of us go upstairs, didn't see either of us leave.'

'It's better than nothing,' said Bognor. 'You could have shinned down the drainpipe, done the business and shinned back up.'

'Yes,' he agreed. 'I didn't, but I could have. I don't think alibi's going to get you very far. I'd move on to motive if I were you.'

'All right,' said Bognor. 'Motive.'

'None,' said the brigadier, smiling. 'Absolutely bugger all.'

'Had you ever met him?'

'Absolutely not,' said the brigadier. '*Pas du tout*. Never clapped eyes on him. Not too keen on sky pilots, if you catch my drift.'

Bognor found himself thinking that the brigadier was too like a brigadier to actually be one. He was reminded of a Simon Raven short story about his caddish anti-hero Fingle impersonating his brigadier during some night exercise. Confronted with the real brigadier, Fingle says that the man must be an impostor because 'his' brigadier wouldn't behave in such a ludicrous self-parodying manner. Faced with Brigadier Blenkinsop, Bognor felt a bit like Fingle. He had known a number of brigadiers in what passed for real life, and most of them had been decent and civilized – unlike this one. Besides, Bognor had always had rather a soft spot for 'sky pilots', coming as he did from a family full of them.

'Known a lot of sky pilots?' he asked.

'Army was full of them,' said the brigadier. 'First-class fighting men, some of them. Absolute shysters, the rest. Come across some in civilian life too. Same problems. One or two absolutely excellent chaps, but the majority complete four-letter men. Don't get me wrong. Religion's all very well in its place, but it doesn't do to let it get in the way of what really matters. The best padres, in my experience, were the ones that put the men first, deferred to people in authority, and kept religion for Sunday morning service. And the occasional funeral. Wedding too, I suppose.'

'So you didn't know Sebastian?'

'Can't say I had the pleasure,' said the brigadier. 'Nothing against the fellow. Doesn't do to speak ill of the dead, either. But I can't help, much as I'd like to. So, if you'll excuse me, I'd better toddle off to keep the little woman company.'

Bognor visualized the prune-like countenance of Esther Blenkinsop, and made a poor fist of suppressing a shudder. Say what you like about Monica, and people did, prunes didn't come into it. He thanked his lucky stars he wasn't married to Mrs Blenkinsop and, come to that, that he wasn't the brigadier, either.

Back at the manor, he found Lady Bognor enjoying just the one or two with their host and hostess.

'How was the Brig?' asked Sir Branwell. 'Lot of hot air, if you ask me. Personally speaking myself, I wouldn't have given him the time of day, but the organizer seems to have the hots for him. Keeps going on about his latest book.'

'What *is* his latest book?' asked Bognor, genuinely not knowing.

The Fludds looked blank. Sir Branwell was colonel-in-chief of the local Yeomanry, some sort of territorial outfit, though he had never seen a shot fired in anger and had missed national service by a year or so. Bognor himself was in much the same boat.

'Heroics,' said Monica, who had actually read it. 'A study in gallantry through the ages, with particular relevance to the Victoria Cross.'

'Ah,' said Sir Branwell. 'One of my ancestors had a VC. Boer War. Killed him. Awarded posthumously to his widow. Dashed stupid. Keep your head down and don't volunteer. That's my advice. Tallisker?'

Bognor didn't mind if he did.

'He's talking about it tomorrow morning,' said Monica brightly.

'His latest book?' said Camilla, beadily.

'Well,' said Monica, 'heroics, heroism, heroes. All that.'

'Same thing,' said Sir Branwell. 'They all do it. Don't blame them in a way, even if they ought to be at home writing, not out on the stage spouting at a whole lot of elderly spinsters who would be better off at home reading. That's the trouble with these literary festivals. They're a substitute for the real thing. Writer chappies not writing, and readers not reading. Won't stop them all gabbing on about it later, though. Certain sort of pseudo-intellectual, particularly. They won't actually read the books, but that won't stop them banging on about them as if they had actually studied every word. If I had my way I'd ban them.'

'That's a bit harsh, Brannie,' said Bognor. 'They give a lot of people harmless pleasure, and they bring in punters and income.'

'That's what everyone thinks,' he said morosely. 'It's not like that at all.'

'How so?' In vino veritas, he thought, realizing that the Scotch on top of the calva was making him decidedly squiffy, and wondering how much his host had had to drink.

'People like little Glasgow call the shots,' said Branwell. 'We're just Aunt Sallies for everyone to take pot shots. Get all the blame, none of the credit, and reap no rewards. Everyone knows Flanagan Fludd was a complete charlatan. No talent, whatever.'

'Vicenza Book said he cribbed off Gilbert and Sullivan.'

'Fat lot she knows about,' he said. 'Nothing but a jumped-up barmaid's daughter. Not that there's anything wrong with being a barmaid's daughter. Someone has to be, I suppose, but just don't go jumping about pretending to be something else.'

'Would she have known Sebastian?'

'Dunno. Probably not. Mother must have done, though. Sebby preached about her. Main reason she left. You could say. Sex and alcohol. She was for sin and Sebastian was against it. They were on opposite sides of the moral divide. The vicar won. People like him always do. It's a matter of morality, which means a question of hypocrisy. That means that in private they approve of people like Vicenza Book's mother; Dolly's ma. In public, though, they side with the vicar. The devil has all the best tunes, but people don't like to be seen dancing to them.'

He poured himself another Scotch, ignored the others, and earned a sharp and censorious glance from his wife.

'Much better now that the Kraut chef's in charge,' he said. 'Bloody awful scoff, but neat and gets a good press.'

'Swiss,' said Camilla. 'Gunther is Swiss.'

'Swiss, piss,' said Sir Branwell laughing. 'Typical Swiss. Neat, tidy and ultimately unimaginative. All cuckoo clocks and yodelling.'

'That's the Austrians,' said Bognor. 'They invented the cuckoo clock and taught the world to yodel.'

'Swiss,' said Sir Branwell very seriously. 'Camilla's quite right. Gunther Battenburg is Swiss. Nothing to do with cake or the royal family. But say what you like about the Swiss, they're very neat and tidy. Their trains run on time and I don't believe the Austrians had anything to do with cuckoo clocks or yodelling. That was the Swiss. Orson Welles said so. And he was spouting the words of Graham Greene. He should know.'

Bognor frowned. He was not following his host's train of thought.

'I may not enjoy his grub,' said Sir Branwell, 'but I applaud his neatness. Everything's always very tidy. No cause for complaint.'

'I didn't think a lot of the dinner was terribly good,' said Bognor. 'Though, I quite liked the emu. Vicenza Book thought it was chicken.'

'She would,' said Sir Branwell. 'Part of the problem with that trollop,' he continued, 'is that she's a mess. No concept of straight lines, order, cleanliness, places and people being in the right place at the right time. Say what you like about the services, they always have a timetable, and everyone adheres to it. Too much civilian life is chaotic.'

Bognor, who enjoyed chaos, which was usually more apparent than real, did not demur, even though he knew that his old friend's knowledge of military life was perfunctory and almost entirely vicarious. On the other hand, the affairs of the Lord Lieutenancy were regulated with a precision which owed much to the armed forces, if not to the Swiss.

'So, I do most profoundly hope,' said Sir Branwell, 'that you can bring something Swiss to the current investigations. If you see what I mean. And by Swiss, I don't mean cheese with holes in it, but clocks, clockwork, tickety-boo.' And he tapped his nose.

'The brigadier doesn't have a satisfactory alibi,' said Bognor, 'but then hardly anybody does. It's going to introduce a bit of a mess into the proceedings, like it or not. On the other hand, he doesn't have a discernible motive, so I'm inclined to rule him out.'

'Talked to the pathologist?' The squire was full of surprises. Bognor suspected he didn't know what a pathologist was, except for what he had gleaned from TV. This meant a sexy girl in a white coat with a scalpel. His own experience with pathologists was not similar. In his experience, they were slightly desiccated males who felt they knew best. On the whole, they tended to tell you what you knew already, but attached much importance to their findings and believed they solved everything. This was not a view Bognor shared.

'The pathologist will tell me that death was by hanging; that the rope and the stool came from the vestry; and that the removal of the stool precipitated death. The pathologist's report will not, however, tell me who tied the knot nor who kicked the stool.'

'Fingerprints?' enquired Sir Branwell. 'DNA?'

'Possible,' said Bognor. 'But even if so, they won't stand up in court. The probability is that Sebastian knew where the rope and the stool were, that he tied the requisite knots and kicked the stool from under him, himself. But there is always the possibility that another party was involved. Or parties. The two questions that need answering are: "Who tied the knot?" and "Who kicked the stool?"'

'Quite,' echoed Sir Branwell.

'I think,' said Monica, 'it's time we all went to bed.'

In situations such as this, Lady Bognor was not to be gainsayed.

'I quite agree,' said Lady Fludd. 'It's quite late; we've all had more than enough to drink and we have a heavy day tomorrow.'

The two men exchanged rheumy glances, but said nothing, simply drained their glasses, and stood unsteadily.

They both knew far better than to argue.

SEVENTEEN

The pathologist was male, of a certain age, sexless and self-important. All this accorded with Bognor's expectations. The pathologist was, naturally, convinced that his report would provide all the answers anyone could possibly want. That, too, was in line with what Bognor expected. Nothing untoward, nothing helpful. Boxes were ticked, protocol followed, and if there had to be a post-mortem examination of a post-mortem examination, so to speak, then everyone would be satisfied that this section of the book had been followed to the letter.

'The time of death was some time between five and seven,' said the pathologist.

Bognor nodded but said nothing. He knew that already but he wasn't saying anything. It made sense for the pathologist to feel that he was providing special information, to which he alone was privy, and could not be discovered by any other means. 'The cause of death was strangulation. This was achieved by hanging by the neck, and the weapon was a spare rope for one of the bells. It almost certainly came from the vestry, as did the stool, which was removed, leaving the dead man dangling from the rafter around which the rope was fixed by means of a bowline knot. The knot around the neck was a common or garden reef.'

'And was the stool removed by the deceased or a third party.'

'Impossible to say.' The pathologist still appeared self-satisfied and portentous, as if this failure to identify the person who had removed the stool was itself something which could only be ascertained by some arcane process, to which he alone was privy.

'And how would you say the stool was toppled. It was on its side was it not?'

'Correct,' said the pathologist. 'I would judge that the

stool was kicked over either by the deceased, using his own feet, or by a third party. We could find no trace of finger-prints or of anything that would show up in DNA testing. My guess is that the stool was knocked over by a shoe or a boot. It's impossible to say, and shoes and boots leave no trace.'

'Guess?' said Bognor. 'No trace? That doesn't sound the sort of scientific evidence that will stand up in a court of law.'

The pathologist shifted from one foot to another. A certain sort of novelist would have said this was a symptom of unease, but the pathologist still seemed very pleased with himself and his evidence, though Bognor could not see why. He seldom could.

'No,' said the pathologist, 'we can only go so far.'

'I thought pathology was an exact science,' said Bognor mischievously.

'Only as far as it's allowed to be scientific. The moment we enter the realm of speculation, we're as tentative and unrigorous as everyone else.'

'My view,' said Bognor evenly, 'is that pathology is always as tentative and unrigorous as everyone else. However, because it is possible to dress up your proceedings in formulaic scientific language, it is possible for you to fool people. You don't, however, fool me. I also think that there is a natural ghoulishness in a lot of laymen, which is obsessed with knives and body parts, dissection and what passes for forensics. I believe much of what you do to be so much fashionable mumbo-jumbo, but I am not usually allowed to say so.'

'I was warned you were old-fashioned,' said the patholo-gist, taking umbrage. 'I hadn't realized you were prehistoric.'

Bognor shrugged. He was past caring.

'Listen sunshine,' he said, wishing he were with his wife and the Fludds listening to the brigadier bark on equally ludicrously about a subject on which he was no expert either, but making it sound, by dint of slides, statistics and sundry other devices, as if he knew what he was talking about,

'you do your job and I'll do mine.' On reflection, the brigadier and the pathologist had a great deal in common,
pretending to a level of expertise which was essentially
bogus, but relying on it, and sundry more or less false
qualifications, to claim a level of competence which excluded
the common man. This included people such as Bognor.
Bognor, however, had the advantage of an Apocrypha education, an enquiring mind and the ability to cut through the
sort of crap offered up by the pathologist and the brigadier.
Give him a good generalist, any time. Which was not to
say that he didn't acknowledge the place of the genuine
authority, but they were few and far between, and life was
dogged by the half-baked, semi-qualified – such as the
brigadier and the pathologist – masquerading as experts,
when in fact they knew a great deal less than men of the
world, such as Simon.

All this flashed through his mind, as he poured professional
scorn on the pathologist, while heeding warnings about doing
things according to the book of rules, not antagonizing people
such as pathologists without good reason and much else
besides. There was a lot going on beneath those beetling
brows and that affable mildly bovine exterior. Still waters run
deep, and his waters were stiller and ran deeper than anyone,
except possibly his wife, quite realized.

'I shall report you,' said the pathologist. 'I'm not used
to being spoken to like this.'

'More's the pity,' said Bognor before he could help
himself. A still small voice, probably Monica's, was telling
him that they were all in this together and it wouldn't do
to make enemies of one's own team. The voice was running
deep.

'Look,' Bognor was being placatory. He even thought of
putting a hand on the pathologist's shoulder, but decided
against it. The gesture could have been misinterpreted, but
was almost bound to seem inflammatory. 'You and I are
never going to agree. I have your report, for which many
thanks. Now, I shall go off and carry on with my job. You've
done yours and I'm properly grateful.'

'You'll ignore what I said,' complained the pathologist,

obviously far from mollified. 'People like you are all the same. You should have gone out with the Ark.'

'We did,' said Bognor, 'in a manner of speaking. There are very few people like me left. You and your kind are the masters now.'

'Not before time.' The pathologist spoke with feeling. 'Our job is to present cold scientific facts about which there can be no argument. We don't allow ourselves the luxury of arty-farty feelings and speculation, much less intuition, as you seem to call it. People like you fly by the seat of your pants, which is an apt simile if you ask me. Seat of your pants is exactly what you're all about.'

'It's a metaphor not a simile,' said Bognor, 'though I wouldn't expect you to know the difference. Nor care, even if you knew.' This was a proverbial red rag to the equally proverbial bull, and he knew it. But he couldn't care less.

'So, who do you think did it?' asked the pathologist.

'I don't know,' said Bognor, truthfully.

The pathologist looked at him sceptically.

'But you think you know,' he said, eventually. It was said accusingly.

'No,' said Bognor, 'at the moment I simply don't have the foggiest. But, unlike some people, I have an open mind. And I value that. And I shall endeavour to hang on to it.'

'Meaning?'

'Meaning that I don't.'

'I didn't say that.'

'But you implied it,' said Bognor. 'So who's being unscientific now?'

They glowered at each other. They were involved in some sort of stand-off, and Bognor wondered idly, as was his wont, whether or not it was Mexican. If so, then part of the definition was that neither party could win, and the inevitable result was some kind of mutually assured destruction. There was nothing particularly Mexican about a situation such as this. Indeed, a dictionary from another place suggested that the term was invented by Australians who, in this instance, at least, knew absolutely nothing about which they were allegedly talking. His own understanding was that a number of terms had the word Mexican inserted by Americans from north of the border, and that this was nothing more than an expression of racial contempt of the kind habitually used by the English about everyone else. It was merely an expression of superiority. In this instance, it suggested that there was no way out of the situation. There was nothing more Mexican about it than, for instance, a Mexican spit roast, which was a very rude expression, given a racial significance by the fact that the men concerned habitually sported sombreros, which were a form of Mexican national headgear, as distinctive and unusual as the Zapata moustache or tequila.

All this flashed through Bognor's mind, as he realized that he had insulted the pathologist and the only way out was for him to apologize. If he did, the matter should be resolved and the stand-off would cease to be Mexican, in the generally accepted sense.

'I'm sorry,' he said, but the pathologist was not to be defused so easily. As far as he was concerned, the stand-off was indeed Mexican and there was no way out.

'People like you always say things like that,' he said.

'I only apologized.'

'Exactly,' said the pathologist. 'Typical. You think you can be as rude as you bloody well like, and that you can then apologize, which makes it all right. Well, it doesn't. Life isn't like that.'

'No,' said Bognor, feeling even more confused. 'You're right. It isn't. Maybe I should make myself plain.'

'I wish,' said the pathologist.

'What I mean,' said Bognor, sighing inwardly, because he knew this was going to make a bad situation worse, 'is that I believe that murder and its solution is, on the whole, and as a general rule, not a rational matter, and, as such, is not susceptible to rational analysis.'

'I disagree,' said the pathologist.

'Of course you do,' said Bognor, irritating his opponent still more. 'That's your job. I wouldn't expect anything else.'

'Just because murder is usually committed in a non-rational, whimsical manner and for similar reasons, doesn't mean to say that it's not subject to rational scientific laws. That's what my colleagues and I provide.'

'Up to a point,' agreed Bognor. 'But, with respect, it's quite a limited point.'

'What do you mean by that?' The pathologist didn't really want to know. He was buying argumentative moments. Calling an intellectual time out.

'What I mean,' said Bognor speaking very slowly, as if to a foreigner, halfwit or small child, 'is that death isn't about scalpels and dissection, and positions of bodies and times of death; it's about matters of far greater importance and far greater complexity.' He seemed briefly to backtrack but didn't, in fact. 'I concede,' he admitted, 'that people, such as yourself, have a part to play in an investigation such as this, but it's a small part, a subsidiary part and not even necessarily a relevant part.'

'I don't agree,' said the pathologist, desperately.

'Well, if you think you can tell who killed the Reverend Sebastian Fludd because of what you have found in his stomach, or the sort of knot used to tie the rope to the beam, or to any one of a number of sexy but silly things you have discovered because of your so-called scientific procedures, then you are even more ridiculous than I think you are. Thank you for your report, which is required by law and by convention, and will no doubt make very interesting reading, but will be of no help whatever in determining who killed the dead man or why.'

'You . . . you . . . amateur,' said the pathologist, making the word sound as insulting and pejorative as he could. It would only have been worse if he had inserted the word Mexican as a qualifying adjective.

'Well, on that note,' said Bognor, 'it only remains for me to take formal delivery of your report, to take official cognizance of what you say, and to assure you that your professional competence will be noted in the usual and correct manner. I may say, in passing, that nothing you have said or written is of the slightest use or relevance to my enquiries. Nevertheless, I acknowledge, that for all sorts of reasons, I am required to listen to what you say and to read your findings. This I have done, this I shall do, but I have more important things to do, and so, without more ado, I will say, again, thank you very much, leave you to your own devices and see myself out.'

Which he did.

He felt he had won the battle, but he was very much afraid he had lost the war.

EIGHTEEN

Martin Allgood, the once trendy, once sexy, once promising writer-in-residence, was Bognor's next interviewee. He reminded Bognor of a footballer who had once been on the books of Arsenal or Manchester United, but had never entirely lived up to his transfer fee, and was now eking out his days playing for someone like Scunthorpe United or Crewe Alexandra, which, in many respects, the Fludd Literary Festival resembled. Inwardly, Sir Simon allowed himself a quiet chuckle at the notion of the Fludd Festival as the bookish equivalent of Crewe Alexandra. He corrected himself in mid-laugh, however – more like Plymouth Argyle, with Allgood in the role of Paul Mariner. That, though, was inaccurate and unfair to many of those concerned. Mariner was the manager, after all, and Bognor had once seen him in his pomp, as the striker of a high-flying Ipswich Town. Martin Allgood had never had a pomp – only promise. Still, he reminded Bognor of a footballer who had never quite made the grade. Not unlike the brigadier. Once upon a time, the brigadier had kept a field marshal's swagger stick hidden promisingly in his knapsack. However, he had never had occasion to use it once he had been passed over as a mere brigadier. It was a bit the same with Allgood. No Nobel Prizes for him; nor even an evening with Candia McWilliam and Colin Thubron at the Royal Society of Literature or PEN. Martin Allgood was a bit of an also-ran, which was why, let's face it, he was the Writer-in-Residence at the Fludd Festival of Literature and the Arts.

It didn't seem to have dented his self-confidence, however. Better a big fish in a small pond, than no sort of fish at all. And his publicist may have been ignorant and stupid, but her breasts were pert and her cheekbones high, and she was probably very good in bed. Good enough for Martin Allgood, anyway, and she was all his, at least for the duration of the festival. She came with the board, the lodging and the billing, all of which were of a tolerably high order, even if the Fludd Festival wasn't in the Premiership, even if the eponymous Flanagan had been a bit of a fraud, even if Allgood wasn't even, truth be told, good enough to be superannuated. As he had said at dinner: 'Beats work.'

He didn't like the clergy any more than the brigadier, but he didn't call them 'sky pilots', referring to them instead, quaintly, as 'God botherers'. This signified his background of minor public school ('Kimbolton, actually'), decent but unfashionable red-brick university (Hull) and a moderate chip on the shoulder. Incidentally, he claimed to have been a protégé of Philip Larkin at Hull, and there seemed to be no one willing or able to contradict him, least of all Larkin, who was dead.

So, he didn't care much for 'God botherers', though you could take them or leave them, even though he was inclined to leave them, and, no, he hadn't known the late reverend, and he was, natch, sorry, the old stiff had snuffed it, but there you go, one of those things he supposed, and it wasn't, after all, quite as bad for God botherers who believed in a life after death, unlike most people, and the Reverend Sebastian could at least bother God in person, tweak his long white beard, make fun of the long white socks he stuffed into his Clarks' sandals and the aerated white bread with which he made his Marmite sandwiches. Heaven was, he was reliably informed by those who knew, full of long white beards, Clarks' sandals and Marmite sandwiches. A bit like an old British Rail waiting room in a station where you changed on to a picturesque railway line destined for hiking country. 'Carlisle, eh . . . all change for Settle. Cool, eh?'

The publicist's name was Tracey, he thought. Could be Kelley. Or Britney. It ended in 'ey'. He was pretty certain about that. More hairdresser than publisher, he agreed, even in the publicity department, though nowadays you couldn't really tell the difference, and she was good in bed, which was where they had been yesterday between five and seven, in the four-poster in Azalea, with a bottle of bubbly, and, cool, eh?, and he supposed we only had Tracey or Kelley or Britney's word for it, which wasn't a lot to go on, but it was all he had, so there it was. Unless you can count room service, but they had brought up the champagne nearer four than five, which he remembered because it was well before the final football results on TV, and Stoke did really well, he had always supported them since he was at school. Cool. He used the word a fair bit, which dated him more than a bit, and was the day before yesterday's word, just as he was the day before yesterday's writer, if he had a period, but if you really wanted to know the best was yet to come, and he was working on something right now, which was going to be well, er, well, maybe he was going to say 'cool', but that was a word he'd been caught out for using at least once before, and it wouldn't happen again, if he could help it, know what I mean?

Talked a lot, Martin Allgood.

'So, you'd never met the vicar?' asked Bognor, during one of the infrequent lulls in the monologue.

Allgood couldn't say he had, though he'd clapped eyes on him a couple of times out and about, seeing as he, Allgood, had already been in Mallborne a day or two, organizing workshops in the school, and for the local writers' group who met every Thursday evening and had been reading *Rubbish* as their set text. *Rubbish* was the book which Monica had asked about, and which had confirmed Allgood's promise and secured him his place among the twenty most promising British writers of his generation. It had appeared quite a long time ago.

'I'm afraid I haven't read *Rubbish*,' admitted Bognor.

'Me neither,' said Allgood. 'Nor what's her face, though she isn't exactly into books, really. The ladies from the writers' group had read it, though. All of them. Seemed to like it, too. Asked all sorts of intelligent questions. But they seemed a bit disappointed when I told them I didn't know what the most important six rules of successful best-seller writing were. They had Jeffrey Archer down a month or so ago, and he reeled them straight off pat, then repeated them word for word, so they could take notes.'

For a moment, Allgood looked almost wistful at the thought of Jeffrey Archer's six rules of successful best-seller writing, about which he had known so distressingly little. Then he brightened.

'Do you reckon he topped himself, or got someone else to do the dirty deed? Or was it a hostile third party?' he asked, and sat back, expecting some sort of answer.

'The convention is,' Bognor said stiffly, 'that I ask the questions and you answer them. That's the way it is.'

He was painfully aware that he was sounding pompous, so tried lightening the mood. 'That's what the book says,' he said. 'It's a bit like the Jeffrey Archer rules of best-seller writing. If you play according to the rules, you do as the rules say.' He lowered his voice. 'I'm afraid, though,' he conceded, 'that I'm not awfully clever when it comes to rules. I can never remember what they're supposed to be, and when I do remember, I tend to pay no attention.'

'Bit like me,' said Allgood. 'Effort and sweat, and all that kind of stuff, is a bit of a nuisance, as well. Don't care for that, either.'

'No,' Bognor agreed, 'I know what you mean.' He thought for a moment. Then, as if coming to a momentous decision, he said, 'To be absolutely honest, at the moment, I don't have a clue who did it. I just have a feeling that someone did.'

'Well,' said Allgood, 'he's dead, isn't he? These things don't just happen.'

'I don't know so much,' said Bognor, 'he could have had a stroke or a heart attack. These things happen. Act of God. Takes everyone by surprise. Most of all the dear, dead departed.'

'And if it were a stroke or a heart attack,' said Allgood, apparently thinking out loud, 'the death would have a certain elegant appropriateness. A bit like one's employer suddenly firing one. I mean, if God wanted to fire one of his workers, he wouldn't have to fire them, he'd just reel them in. Wasn't He supposed to be a fisher of men?'

'I hadn't thought of it like that,' said Bognor, truthfully. He hadn't. 'So, you're telling me you didn't kill the vicar,' he said after a pause.

Allgood seemed to give the idea his full attention, worrying at it like a dog with one of those bone-shaped toys. Eventually, he said, 'I don't see that I did. I mean, why?

You need some sort of a reason. I grant you, I had the opportunity, because you wouldn't trust the sexy little hair-dresser further than you could throw her, if you see what I mean. But you need some kind of motive, and I don't think I have one. I could probably make one up, mind. That's what I'm paid to do.' He brightened. 'We could make it the main topic of my next workshop. Think of a motive for my murdering the vicar. That would be fun.'

'Not especially,' said Bognor. 'In fact, you could even argue that doing so would be obstructing the course of justice.'

'In which case, you'd be completely justified in throwing the book at me,' said the writer, 'except that it sounds suspiciously like a book of rules. The sort of thing someone like Archer would have put together. And you don't believe in rule books and things like it. So you'd be unlikely to throw it at me.'

'Touché,' said Bognor, wondering momentarily if he should read *Rubbish*. Monica hadn't ventured an opinion on it, though it was not in her nature to finish books she didn't like. Nor to begin them without a serious recommendation from someone she trusted.

'Interesting,' said Allgood, as if he had only just realized that the death of the vicar raised questions that ought to be answered. Not questions that had a desperate need to be answered, especially if you felt like the squire and valued orderliness above justice. If, on the other hand, you were naturally anarchic and had a belief in right and wrong, however laid back and unconventional that might be, then the sudden death of the Reverend Fludd posed questions that could be amusing to answer. Particularly in a closed society at a time like this.

'I'd like to see it all debated,' said Allgood. 'Not least because I can think of any one of a number of people who would like to see no such thing.'

'Hmmm.' Bognor looked at the writer with an interest which bordered on affection. He found himself in broad agreement.

'You believe in entertainment, not in justice?'

'Something like that,' said Allgood. 'Though, I don't see that the two are necessarily exclusive. If you can have entertaining justice, I'm doubly in favour. My sense is that most people are keener on boring injustice. I'd never thought of the truth being fun, but I'm beginning to think I may be wrong. In this case, it could be rather merry to overturn a few conventional apple carts in the search for a murderer. And if you decided to pull a decent veil over the whole affair and say that the Reverend Sebastian knocked himself off while the balance of his mind was disturbed, that could be awfully dull.'

'Neat though?'

Allgood thought some more, a process which required an effort he obviously did not enjoy.

'I don't think I do neat,' he said at length. 'Truth, justice and all that stuff strike me as a bit prissy, but neatness is really uncool.'

It was Bognor's turn to think for a while.

Eventually he said, 'You may just have given me a motive.'

'How so?' the author wanted to know.

'You could have killed the vicar in order to cause mischief,' he said. 'To create disorder.'

'Sounds a bit extreme,' said Allgood, 'but worth a thought. Worth a thought.'

NINETEEN

Dorcas was tearful.

This was only to be expected, but it did not make the occasion any easier. Bognor hated talking to the newly bereaved and simply didn't buy into the widely held belief that such meetings were in any sense therapeutic. In his experience, which was considerable, they were invariably sticky, seldom very relevant and nearly always yielded unpleasant and unexpected new truths.

Dorcas was plain, which, he supposed, didn't help, and her skin was mottled from grief and tears. She was not dressed in widow's weeds, but in various drab colours and shapes that Bognor assumed were par for her course, and had little or nothing to do with her recent loss.

'I'm sorry,' he said, sitting down in a high-backed Victorian armchair. The cottage was comfortable enough, but had an air of impermanence which suggested that it went with the job and was not the vicar's own. He presumed it was also in Sir Branwell's gift. 'I know this is a difficult time.'

Clichés were often the best way of dealing with such interviews. They were like the traditional form of church service. They had been around a long time and carried the patina of familiarity. They had also withstood the test of former use. They worked, which was why they were still trotted out.

'I quite understand,' she said. 'You have a job to do. Would you like tea? Or something stronger? A glass of sherry, perhaps?'

Tea or sherry were also ritual comforts in such situations, and had been for almost as long as the verbal clichés. They were almost as much of a British middle-class response as *Hymns Ancient and Modern* or the *Book of Common Prayer*. They were invaluable crutches in much the same way, and owed as much to their familiarity as to any therapeutic or medicinal properties. When the going gets tough, the tough get going was a popular saying, but the British truism was that when the going gets tough, one turns to tea or sherry, hymns or prayers. Everyone to their own, but it was in this that a certain sort of true Brit found solace.

Bognor said he'd like tea, please. Black, no sugar. A habit he had picked up many years ago on a job in Sweden, involving the gift department of NK in Stockholm. Fre Roos had called him in after representations had been made by the man who handled the British side of the store's business. Wrapping paper had played a crucial part in the business and he was helped inordinately by his command of the English language, which was even better than that of the average Swede. The average Swede spoke better English than the average Englishman, but Bognor also spoke better English than the average Englishman.

'No,' he said, 'just as it comes.' He actually preferred artisan's tea – strong and robust, with no messing around with milk or exotic fruit. He wasn't in the least interested in the crucial debate, which meant so much to so many of his compatriots, about whether the milk went in first or last. He couldn't be holding with effeminate additions when it came to tea.

Dorcas poured from a capacious black teapot and he was relieved to discover that the liquid was Typhoo, scaldingly hot. He had feared he was in for tepid Earl Grey.

'You found him,' said Bognor, sipping. 'That must have been a terrible shock.'

She seemed to consider this for a while, and then said, 'Not really. Sebastian said he'd be back for an early supper around six thirty. I'd made macaroni cheese. He was fond of my macaroni cheese. He used to say that it was what he had married me for.'

She sniffled, and dabbed at her eyes and nose with a rather weedy handkerchief. Bognor felt that a true gentleman would have reached in his breast pocket and offered a sturdier one of his own. For all sorts of reasons, he failed to do this, but let her tell her story in her own way.

'He hadn't been himself recently,' she said. 'Not really. Not the old Sebastian. Not quite the man I knew and loved.'

'In what way?'

Once more, she seemed to be thinking about the question for the first time, even though it was obviously one which she had asked herself many times. Eventually, she said, 'I'd never seen a dead body before. Sebastian was my first. I hope he's my last. He seemed so, well, dead. Somehow, he wasn't what I'd expected. It was the deadness that I found so unexpected. It was as if all the life had gone out of him. I can't really describe it, except to say that he was deader than I had expected. Very dead, indeed.'

'But you say he hadn't seemed himself. What exactly do you mean by that?'

He was beginning to become used to her habit of considering each question as if it was brand new. He found it reassuring.

'He was having doubts,' she said, eventually. 'He'd almost seemed such a black and white person. It was one of the things that I found attractive. He knew what was what. You didn't argue with Sebastian because he had all the answers. He didn't always have the facts or the answers to back them up, but he always knew what he thought. It was true of trivial things too. He never dithered about what he was going to wear. He had very clear likes and dislikes when it came to food and drink.'

Like the macaroni cheese, thought Bognor, saying nothing.

'He didn't like cats,' she said, unexpectedly.

'Didn't like cats,' repeated Bognor feeling foolish. 'More of a dog person.'

'More of a dog person. Definitely more of a dog person.'

'But you didn't have one? A dog.'

'No,' she paused, 'he doesn't . . . I'm sorry . . . didn't really approve of pets.'

'Ah.' The slip into the present tense was quite usual, a

typical problem in coming to terms with sudden loss. The
couple had had no children and now it transpired that
the reverend, though a dog-lover, had not approved of pets.
Poor Dorcas was now completely on her own. Her
husband's death would have left a particularly large hole.
She did not seem to be the sort of person who would have
many friends, let alone influence people. Sadly, she seemed
the sort of person who would pass through life relatively
unnoticed.

'Liked dogs but didn't approve of pets,' said Bognor,
fatuously.

'He thought they were free spirits. Didn't like the idea
of their being domesticated. He thought they were reduced
in some way. I'm not sure I agree.'

'So, you think you might buy a dog.'

She smiled. 'I might,' she said, 'I might.' She sobbed
quietly and then pulled herself together with a shake with
an all too visible effort.

'I'm sorry,' he said, 'I have to ask these questions,
even though I know they're distressing. Can you tell me
why you visited St Teath's? And describe what you found
when you got there and how you reacted.'

At first she was silent, but then she spoke, very softly
and in deliberate sentences with beginnings, middles and
ends, very logical, almost as if rehearsed.

'Sebastian said he wanted to compose his sermon in
church. That was something he always did. He also said he
would be back by six thirty. He was always very good about
things like that. He knew that lateness upset me and I liked
to be early for everything, even the bus.'

She smiled a wan, drab smile and Bognor had a sudden
vision of a long, lonely widowhood stretching out before
her. The Reverend Sebastian was almost certainly the only
man in her life, and he had been reeled in early, leaving
her what might seem like an eternity of solitude. Probably.
He couldn't know for certain. One could never know the
future for certain and maybe not the present, nor the past.
It was his job to try to produce certainty about the past,
to tell it how it really was. At the same time, he was

forced to agree that even his most certain recommend-
ations and findings were more to do with probability than
certainty. Even confessions were partial. One person's
view was not every person's view. If two or three gathered
together and agreed on a certain version of events, that
did not make them more real. Truth was necessarily
elusive. It changed and shifted according to time, whim,
perspective. If three years of Modern History at Apocrypha
had taught him anything, it was the essential partiality of
truth, the elusiveness of justice, the essential 'wrongness'
of the 'right' verdict. There was always another perspective, another point of view, even when the 'facts' seemed
cut and dried.

'So your husband was punctual and thoughtful, liked dogs
but hated pets?'

She smiled. 'That makes him sound, oh, you know . . .'
She broke off, trying to put her late husband into something
approaching perspective. 'Sebastian was a people person
. . .' she said, eventually, and then seemed to be aware that
this was a cliché – possibly comforting, but not true. At
least not necessarily, not everlastingly.

'I think he liked people,' she said, 'no matter what the
state of their beliefs. Or behaviour. He really liked sinners.
In fact, I think he preferred sinners to the righteous. Give
him a good murderer, any day. Virtuous people were a bit
limp and Laodicean for him.'

'He'd have spewed them out?' he ventured.

She caught the biblical allusion and smiled.

'I thought I knew him,' she said. 'Now, I begin to wonder
if I knew him any better than anyone else. I begin to wonder if
anyone really knew him. But, I also begin to wonder
if anyone really knows anyone else. Indeed, I wonder whether
we know ourselves.'

'Probably not,' said Bognor. After all, he hardly knew
himself, so why should anyone else, even Monica?

He realized, dimly, that the interview was wandering out
of control. Spiralling. On the other hand, the best interviews
were like that. Only idiots used clipboards and were not
prepared for apparent inconsequentialities, unexpected

riders, things that went bump and interfered with arguments and prejudices. Even so . . .

'It must have been distressing?'

'Finding him?' She considered the question. 'I suppose so, though not in the way I expected.'

'Expected?'

She seemed surprised that he had picked up on the word.

'I'd thought about it,' she said. 'Doesn't everyone? Life can't go on for ever. We have to be prepared for God doing something we hadn't bargained for.'

'So you think it was an act of God?'

'I think I'm a Christian,' she said, 'and if that's what I am, then everything is in some way an act of God. Isn't that part of being a Christian? We have a bit of free will, but only a bit, and even that's an illusion. God can always override it.'

'You could put it like that,' Bognor agreed. He saw her point of view from deep down, as well as professionally. In that sense, he had to agree with Sir Branwell. What difference, in the great scheme of things, did man's verdict of innocent or guilty mean? Were they absolute concepts? Valid concepts, even?

'You do realize that you were either the last person to see your husband alive or the first person to see him dead.'

'That presupposes that either he committed suicide or that I killed him. It doesn't allow for murder by a third party. If that happened, then the murderer would have been the last person to see him alive and the first person to see him dead.'

'Which was it?'

He felt exasperated. At one moment she seemed almost precociously bright, the next unconscionably dim. There didn't seem to be any half measures.

'The last person to see him alive? Or the first person to see him dead?'

She allowed herself a fleeting smile. 'If I killed dear Sebastian, then the two aren't exclusive. In fact, they're the reverse. If I killed him, then I would be the last person to see him alive and the first to see him dead. If I wasn't the murderer, I wouldn't have seen him alive. Only the body.'

'So which was it? First? Or both? Did you kill him? Did he kill himself? Or was it a third party?'

'You're the professional,' she said sweetly. 'It's for you to decide.'

TWENTY

He was getting somewhere, even though he didn't know where. Even the arrival was far from assured. He felt as if this meandering interrogation was going to end in a conclusion, but he still didn't know what it was, nor even if it would be useful or germane.

He shifted tack.

'Do you think your husband's death had anything to do with the literary festival? Or was it just a coincidence?'

Again she smiled.

'The timing is interesting,' she said. 'If he had died at any other time, it would have been unlikely to attract attention. As it . . . well . . . who can say? Part of your role is to avoid publicity, keep things tidy and orderly, to avoid fuss. On the other hand, I sense that you want to establish the truth. The two may coincide. Or not. Who knows?'

'I don't think that answers my question,' he said. 'One of my problems is to establish whether this tragedy could have occurred at any time, or whether it took place specifically because it was the eve of the festival. What do you think?'

'I don't know,' she said.

'But what do you *think*? Thinking and knowing aren't the same. One is an opinion and the other is a statement of fact. If you can produce the latter, then that's great, but I suspect you can't. In which case, I'll have to make do with something more speculative. Obviously, that's not as helpful, but it's better than nothing.'

'I'm sorry,' she said, 'I really am, but I don't have an opinion.'

He shifted tack again.

'When I talked to the bishop,' he said, 'I got the impression that Sebastian was going through some kind of crisis.

He was suddenly doubting his belief. Personally, I don't see that there is any relation between this crisis of confidence and the festival. I could be wrong, of course, but I don't see any connection. What do you think, though? Was the bishop right? Was the crisis real? Was it significant? Did it have anything to do with the festival. With books? With literature? With being a Fludd?'

Dorcas seemed anguished and confused.

'Ebenezer shouldn't have told you. He only knew about it because he was in a privileged position. It was as if it had been in the confessional. Not that I'm a papist, or anything so vulgar.'

The word 'papist' sounded ludicrously pejorative and old-fashioned to his ecumenical ears. She made 'vulgar' sound vulgar too. He was moderately surprised to hear the bishop referred to with quite such easy familiarity. Three words in about the same number of sentences. He wondered if he was becoming lexicographically threatened.

'Do you think your husband killed himself?' he asked. 'It's a simple question, and you're in the best position to answer. I have to tell you that there is a lot of pressure to decide that he did. It's neater. May not be true, but it's tidy, and why not? If he was murdered by someone else, it's not going to help him. Nothing we do will bring him back.'

'No,' she said, 'I suppose not. He would have preferred it that way.'

'Sorry?' said Bognor, not understanding. 'What would he have preferred and why?'

'He never liked fuss. If he had to be dead, he'd rather just be buried and forgotten. That was his style, and nothing in that respect had changed.'

'What other things had changed?' This time Bognor knew – or thought he knew – what the answer should be. On the other hand, he didn't know whether the widow would want to give it.

There was a long pause, which seemed to confirm his suspicions. Dorcas knew. He knew too, because he had been told by his friend the Rt Rev. Ebenezer. On the other hand, the answer was likely to prove embarrassing and did not necessarily show her in the best light. It might help Bognor, but it could hardly help the Reverend Sebastian. He was beyond help.

'What other things had changed?' he repeated.

'I heard you the first time,' she said. He wondered if she had been similarly crisp with her husband, the vicar. She seemed so mild; a wet blanket of a woman; one of nature's hearth rugs. Women, he thought to himself, were surprisingly deceptive. On the whole, he didn't accept generalizations about the difference between the sexes, not least because Monica, aka Lady Bognor, was not a woman in the accepted sense. Maybe Dorcas Fludd came into a similar category. He doubted it, but all things were possible, especially, he thought ruefully, where women, and more particularly wives, were concerned.

'I'm thinking about your question,' she said, by way of explanation. This did little or nothing to soften the blow. It was probably true and certainly was, in the sense that she had heard the question first time round. His concern was whether she was concocting a plausible lie, or thinking of how best to tell the truth. He was beginning not to trust her.

'Sebastian was having doubts,' she said, confirming what he had already been told by the bishop.

'He doesn't sound the most certain person in the world,' he said. 'I've always found the ability to see several sides of any question appealing.'

She took time to respond to these assertions.

'I know what you mean,' she said eventually, 'and a certain doubtfulness may be attractive in a human being, in a general sense. It's not helpful in a priest. Particularly when it concerns one's vocation.'

'And did it?'

More time for thought. He found this profoundly irritating, but knew that interrupting the silence was playing into her hands. Much better to remain quiet and let her answer his question. She made him wait, but replied in the end. He had no idea whether it was worth the wait, but it was better than nothing and better than interrupting. Of that much he was reasonably sure.

'You could say so,' she said at last. 'Sebastian was having serious misgivings about God.' She smiled wistfully. 'Not clever for a vicar. Sebastian had always shown a remarkably definite belief in the Father Almighty. You could say that this was a necessity. In any event, he used to be rocksteady about that. It was odd, because in almost every other respect, he was a dreadful ditherer. I was the one who took the important decisions. I always acted sensibly and quickly, and I hardly ever changed my mind. Sebastian simply couldn't make his up, except where God was concerned. He always used to be absolutely steady about that, until he changed and religion became as much of a muddle for him as everything else.'

'What exactly do you mean by "everything else"?' he asked, and this time there was no hesitation about the answer.

'Oh, income tax, VAT, church flowers, holy dusters.' She laughed. 'The literary festival. Everything. Life, nuts and bolts.'

'You?' This was daring, intrusive, OTT. He knew this, and saw her mood change immediately. She pinkened.

'He used to be certain about me, much more so than I was about him. I loved him, but I could always see the flaws. The dithering, for instance. He never mentioned my flaws. He always said I was beautiful. He used to believe that I was the best thing that ever happened to him. He accepted the fact that we couldn't have children. But then, at the same time he started to doubt his vocation, he began to doubt me, and to question the nature of love, the sanctity of marriage and,' she became even pinker, 'well, everything.'

'And sex?' Bognor really was pushing his luck now. He knew this, but in for a penny in for a pound, what the hell? The length of her silence and the almost impossible reddening of her cheeks made him think he had, indeed, gone too far, but, to his surprise, she answered, and even though the response was delayed, it was, as far as he could judge, honest. It was certainly explicit.

'We used to have quite a lot of sex,' she said. 'I don't know if we were any good, because we'd only ever known each other in a, well, in a carnal sense. But we suited each other and we enjoyed it. It was meaningful, of course, but fun too. We used to laugh quite a lot in bed. We had a lot of innocent fun. Nothing untoward, I don't think, but tremendous fun.' She grew wistful again. 'Then that stopped. He said it was "wrong", said it was a sin. So, we stopped. For the last few months, we even had separate bedrooms. We never even cuddled. I couldn't help wondering if there was someone else, but I don't think so. It was just him. Or rather not him. He wasn't himself.'

Bognor, inevitably perhaps, thought of himself and Monica. Childless. Faithful. Laughter in bed. Surprisingly sexy. No one else would have suspected. They would have thought it mildly perverse, but then sex was like that. He remembered the sex education talk from his headmaster when he was twelve, and how his best friend had whispered to him incredulously just after, 'Do you realize that he and Mrs Fothergill have actually done that?' It seemed grotesque, quite beyond imagining, but sex was like that. However enjoyable and entertaining it might be for you and your partner, it was unimaginable and mildly disgusting in others. The idea of the late Reverend Sebastian and Dorcas even in a missionary position was either laughable or nauseating, depending on one's viewpoint. At any rate, it was beyond Bognor's ken, just as was his own coupling with Monica.

'So, your husband suddenly developed misgivings about sex and about God,' said Bognor. 'Do you think this sudden access of doubt would have been enough to drive him to take his own life?'

Dorcas seemed to give the idea some thought.

'I wouldn't have said Sebastian was into suicide,' she said. 'You have to be certain of something to kill yourself, and I wouldn't have said Sebby was like that. On the other hand, I would never have believed he could have had second thoughts about God . . . or sex.'

'So, whatever else he may have thought about things, he remained pretty certain about his doubts.'

Simon was rather pleased with this, which while not sufficiently polished to qualify as an aphorism, contained enough unexpectedness to be worth the work. The idea of certainty about doubt was appealing, as well as paradoxical.

'You could say that,' she conceded, 'and in a way, it simply made him a more consistent character. He was in a quandary about absolutely everything, which was not originally the case. It could have driven him to killing himself, though I'd be surprised. On the other hand, his life was full of surprises, so why not his death?'

'Seems a slightly melodramatic way of doing it,' said Bognor. 'He could have taken an overdose, or slit his wrists in the bath.'

'Perhaps he wanted people to notice,' she said. 'Nobody paid much attention to him while he was alive, so why not do a celebrity-style death. It would surprise everyone and possibly draw attention to whatever he wanted people to be drawn to.'

'Which was?' No one had found a note. There was no indication of what he was planning to preach from the pulpit.

'Ebenezer took away his notes for the sermon,' she said as if reading his mind. 'He said it might be helpful and that, in any case, no one else would understand. If they claimed to, they would be guilty of getting everything wrong.'

'How did the bishop get hold of the notes?'

'Sebastian . . .' and then she went pink and checked herself again, 'gave them to him,' she said, after what seemed like another long moment of thought. 'It seemed only right. They were God's business, and it seemed only proper that they should be shared by his servants and not by enemies.'

Bognor made a mental note to ask about the state of Dorcas' own beliefs.

'I hadn't realized that the bishop was on the scene so fast,' he said.

'I didn't say he was,' she said, flustered.

'That's not what I said. Or questioned,' said Bognor.

He supposed he had better have another, perhaps more formal, word with the bishop.

'Does he still have your husband's notes for the sermon?' he asked.

Another silence, and then she nodded. 'I can't think he hasn't,' she said, 'but you'd better ask. I simply don't know.'

'I will,' he said. And he would.

TWENTY-ONE

Monica and the Fludds had been listening to a talk by Martin Allgood. Bognor was working while they played. This was irritating because he had been looking forward to hearing authors speak. On the other hand, it gave him a moral upper hand. That was the theory. Unfortunately, authors, often the least likely, had a habit of getting in the way and saying stuff that was more germane to the puzzle than routine enquiries. That was the reality.

Thus, Allgood.

'Did you know that the Reverend Sebastian had written a book?' asked Sir Branwell. 'Dark horse, Sebby. Provisional title: *The Vicar's Wife*. Taken, I rather fancy, by Trollope minima.'

'Wrong on a number of counts,' said Monica, predictably and crisply. 'Joanna Trollope's book was *The Rector's Wife*, and was inspired by her clerical upbringing in the Cotswolds. And Allgood didn't say Sebastian had written a book. He was being hypothetical.'

'Oh, come on, Monica.' Bognor recognized Branwell's combine-harvester mood, devouring all before him and scattering vegetation and wildlife before him, without serious discrimination. When he took on this guise, he was unstoppable and destroyed everything in his path. 'Little Allgood doesn't do hypothetical. His *oeuvre* is one long *roman-à-clef*, a hymn of self-congratulation.'

'That's unfair,' said Monica, 'and not true, either.' But Sir Branwell was unstoppable. Bognor tried silently warning his wife, flashing his eyes and kicking her under the table. Nothing worked. She stood like an obstinate stook in his path, grass about to be cast to the wind and rendered into featureless chaff. Except that it was unwise to mess with Monica. She was just the sort of rogue blade who would clog otherwise irresistible machinery.

'Don't be ridiculous,' said Sir Branwell, with all the brag-gadocio which had once earned him a congratulatory fourth. 'Little Allgood's never written an original word in his life. It's all faction at best, plagiarism at worst. Everything comes from somewhere else. He just takes real life and makes it boring.'

'Please explain,' said Bognor to all three. 'I am not understanding.'

Camilla Fludd, who had remained silent and seemed to have less of an axe to grind, spoke.

'Allgood spent his entire talk saying what it was like having a novel turned down.'

'Then he can't have been drawing on real life,' said Bognor. 'Allgood's never had a rejection in his life. That's part of his problem.'

'Just because he personally hasn't been turned down,' said Sir Branwell, 'doesn't mean to say that he doesn't know people who have.' He sounded triumphant, like a truculent undergraduate confronted by a particularly dim examiner. 'Don't tell me little Allgood doesn't know all about slush piles and unsolicited manuscripts. Just because it hasn't happened to him.'

'I'm sorry,' said Bognor, aware that he was sounding petulant, 'but nobody has told me what he actually said. All I know is that you all agree that it was good. Branwell said it was based on fact; Monica says it wasn't. But what exactly was it?'

'He said,' said Camilla, 'that rejection was enough to drive someone to drink. Or suicide. Or worse.'

'What could be worse than suicide?' he asked. 'I mean, that's as bad as it gets.'

'Killing someone else is worse than killing oneself. At least, it is in fiction. It may be different in real life, but Allgood is about novels. It's what he does.' This was Camilla again. The other two glowered and said nothing.

'So where did the vicar come in?'

'Allgood brought him in,' said Camilla.

'He didn't have to,' said Branwell. 'I'm afraid Sebastian brought himself in. Evidently, he had written a novel and he couldn't take the constant rejection. Being Sebastian, he went about it all in completely the wrong way and naturally failed to see it, which is why he strung himself up. So, ergo, I was right all the time. He strung himself up. Admittedly, I failed to guess the reason for his topping himself, but I'm afraid that's not the point. He was responsible and he alone. All jolly sad. But no need for any more fuss than deep regret and a proper funeral. New padre needed, but that's another matter. Allgood hit the nail on the head, I'm afraid.'

'With respect,' said Monica, 'that's not what he said. Everything was prefixed with doubt and speculation. He kept saying "if" and "let us suppose". He may have been putting a prosecution case, but that's all. He certainly wasn't putting forward facts. There was absolutely nothing he said which would stand up in court.'

'But *had* the vicar written a book?' asked Bognor.

'Yes,' said Sir Branwell.

'No,' said Bognor's wife.

'We can't be sure,' said Camilla.

'One speech,' said Bognor, 'an audience of three and three completely different interpretations. I'm afraid that, in my experience, that's entirely usual. It doesn't matter how many witnesses you have. It doesn't matter if each one has qualifications to pass themselves off as a trained observer, you are likely to have three completely different versions of what actually happened. That's one reason truth is so difficult to ascertain. Basically, there's no such thing. One man's fact, is another man's fiction; one man's truths are another man's lies. And so it goes on. That's why there is no such thing as real history, why it's possible to have a Marxist interpretation and a Christian one, why it is possible to be Arthur Bryant and tell our island history entirely in terms of kings and queens, or be Christopher Hill and tell the same story as if the only real people involved were diggers and levellers. There is no such thing as objectivity. Never was, never will be. Fact of life.'

'That's what they taught you at Apocrypha?' asked Monica, not really expecting a straight answer and not receiving one.

'Maybe, maybe not,' said her husband. 'Case rests.'

'I don't see that what we were taught at university makes a blind bit of difference,' said Sir Branwell. 'The fact of the matter is that the vicar wrote a novel, had it turned down by a number of publishers, and killed himself as a result. Little Allgood says it happens all the time.'

'Just because it happens all the time,' said Bognor, 'doesn't mean it happened here. What was the vicar supposed to have written?'

'Doesn't make a blind bit of difference,' said Branwell. 'Could have been Shakespeare, Dickens, Hardy and Jane Austen rolled in one, for all the industry cared, and for all the difference it made to the poor fellow's disillusion and suicide. He went about it completely the wrong way: didn't have an agent, probably submitted a photograph of himself in a dog collar, which said middle-class, middle-aged, Caucasian male failure. Wouldn't be surprised to find he sent a picture of himself with a beard. I'm not a celebrity get me out of here. Except that, he was never even in it. Wherever "it" is.'

'What if the book was any good?' asked Bognor innocently.

'You don't suppose anyone actually read it?' Sir Branwell was incredulous. 'Never had a lot of time for little Allgood, but he talked a lot of sense today. The vicar's book would have gone straight into the slush pile and stayed there until someone sent him a rejection slip. No one would have read it. They don't read books nowadays. Probably can't. That's what Allgood said. You can learn a thing or two at a good literary festival like ours. Beats reading any day.'

'Everything seems to beat reading these days,' said Monica. She was obviously spoiling for a fight. 'Including so-called literary festivals. You've heard the author plugging his latest book, so you don't have to bother reading it. Dead vicar at end of rope in own church; don't read all about it; just listen to Martin Allgood being speculative. Honestly.' She was very angry.

'I don't see the problem,' said Bognor. 'We only have to ask Dorcas if Sebastian had written a novel. Either way, I don't see rejection as a motive. Thousands of people have books rejected.'

'Most of them unread,' said Sir Branwell with an air of triumph.

'What if Sebastian had written a good book?' Bognor was being *faux naif*, but it was a perfectly legitimate question. It was unlikely that the vicar had written a good book, whatever that might be, and the semi-plagiarism of the title was a bad augury. Nevertheless, the idea was possible, and Bognor was not a man to leave a stone unturned. If he did, it might gather moss, he told his long-suffering subordinates whenever the opportunity arose.

Sir Branwell was exultant. 'In the unlikely event that little Sebastian had written a good book, it would have been even less likely to find a publisher.'

Even Bognor found this a little over the top, but the squire was now in full flight.

'Sebby being Sebby would have sent the manuscript off with all conceivable strings left unpulled. His typescript would therefore have gone straight on to the slush pile. There it would have remained for the requisite number of months, before the book would have been returned in the stamped addressed envelope so thoughtfully provided. Without an sae, it would just have been thrown out. Just possible it would have been picked up by some typist, who might have taken it home to read, might conceivably have enjoyed it, might possibly have put in a recommendation to that effect. If she did, which would be very unlikely, her bosses would have ignored it. They always do. It's in the job description.'

'There's no such thing as a typist these days,' said Monica, still combative. 'They all have laptops, even the super bosses, even if they don't know how to use them.'

Sir Branwell ignored her.

'Had Sebastian been a celebrity of some description – a cook, say, or a supermodel – he might have stood a chance. But he was a common-or-garden middle-aged man with a dog collar, and more hair on his chin than the top of his head.'

This was true, metaphorically at least, so Monica kept shtum but looked mulish.

'Not a chance, poor bugger. And the reasons were completely beyond his purlieu, let alone control. And after two or three, or even more, such rejections he was feeling a bit down. Only human nature. Even for a man of God. Maybe particularly, for a man of God.'

He looked round, evidently thinking he had scored a great victory and talked lots of sound common sense.

'I still don't see any evidence that the vicar had written a book at all. Still less submitted it to a publisher; even less had it rejected several times and been driven to suicide.'

'It's happened to better men than the Reverend Sebastian Fludd,' said Sir Branwell, portentously. 'Established authors; men of letters; anybody lacking celebrity status. I wouldn't be surprised if even little Allgood had had his problems.'

'Precisely,' said Monica, pouncing. This was her moment and she seized it. 'Little Allgood is getting a bit long in the tooth; he's past it; he has trouble staying in flight; which is why he was so keen on using the vicar as a hypothetical example.'

'Talking of long in the tooth,' said Branwell, 'you have to admire the man's gnashers. They must have cost a pretty penny. That's a lot of copies.'

'That's Amis not Allgood,' said Monica, who liked to keep up with matters literary, even when they concerned dentistry. 'He's in danger of becoming a grumpy old man, but he's not like Allgood. Not remotely. And certainly not when it comes to teeth or slush piles.'

'I still thought he spoke awfully well,' said Camilla, managing to miss several points at the same time. 'I felt really sorry for poor Sebastian. I mean how could they?'

'I feel sorry for him too,' said Bognor. 'He's dead.'

'And however well Allgood spoke, and however much everyone huffs and puffs about whether or not he was being hypothetical or not, neither of you is going to bring him back. Much better to do as I said, draw a line in the sand and get on with things. It's what he would have wanted after all. No use crying over spilled milk or hanged vicars. These things happen. Life has to go on.'

It was on the tip of his tongue to say that they had had

this argument before, but Bognor thought better of it, buttoned his lip, which was stiffish, and gave very little away. Privately, however, he decided it would be sensible to have another word with Martin Allgood, and to establish whether or not he knew more of the deceased than he had previously been letting on. After all, Bognor reckoned he was the only one present who had read Allgood – the aptly named *Minimal Expectations*, which had Dickensian echoes and more than a little Dickensian hubris.

TWENTY-TWO

Before talking to Allgood again, Sir Simon had to phone the office. Harvey Contractor, his ambitious, talented, overqualified sidekick was manning the place in his boss's absence, and it was to him that Bognor spoke. He was so immersed in the English countryside and the death of the vicar, that he had almost forgotten that Contractor existed.

'Thick plot already,' he said. 'But getting thicker by the moment.'

Contractor had a degree, a good one, in semiotics from the University of Wessex in Casterbridge. His boss pretended not to know what this meant. Contractor humoured him in this, as in most respects. One day, Bognor's job would be his. No competition. All he had to do was bide his time and keep his nose clean.

'Anything you say, boss.'

'This is supposed to be a holiday,' said Bognor, trying not to whinge. 'It's anything but. I'm working flat out. Bloody hideous.'

Contractor yawned. The phone call had interrupted his 'fiendishly difficult' Sudoku. Contractor habitually finished it fast. He himself could be fiendishly difficult when he wanted, but he tried not to be with Bognor. He rather liked the old thing and saw through the veil of assumed stupidity which, on the whole, Sir Simon wore lightly. It did not fool Contractor, nor really was it meant to.

Contractor had read the whole of Proust in the original French, being averse to translation, and being able to read in a lot of languages. He was weaned on Simenon, also in French, and was an expert on crime literature from Bulgaria, Flanders and Finland. He was fluent on Thomas Merton and early Coetzee. He had fingered Henning Mankell as an emerging talent before anyone else in Britain was aware of him, and he had learned to despise Dan Brown similarly early on. He was, in short, literaturely perspicacious and he didn't do festivals. He believed that writers should be read and not heard. Had he been at the Fludd, he might have heckled.

'Problem?' he asked.

'Routine,' said his boss. 'Quick trip to Kew. Check out the army list in the National Archives. I want you to cast an eye over the Mobile 13th in the sixties. See if there are any familiar names there.'

'That's Blenkinsop's old regiment, isn't it?'

'Could be.' Contractor was right. He nearly always was. It was the main reason he was hired.

'OK. Can you tell me what I'm looking for?'

'I could, but I won't.' Bognor smiled and laughed inwardly. If the information he was seeking was there, Contractor would find it. He was damned, though, if he was going to give his subordinate the satisfaction of knowing this. Bad enough to have someone as cocky as Contractor working for him; worse still to encourage him.

Contractor laughed back. He understood the rules of the game only too well. 'Your call, boss,' he said. 'I'll get down to Kew and call you back. Remember me to Lady B.' He laughed again. He and Monica had a good relationship; flirtatious, competitive, but mutually respectful as well. Quite right.

Actually, Bognor rather liked Harvey Contractor, which those who thought he was more conventional than he actually was might have found peculiar. Sir Branwell, who referred to Harvey, in a faux-jocular way, as 'Your nig-nog', affected to find the affection odd, but Bognor was completely without the usual prejudices of middle-class, middle-aged, white English males. He knew that a certain sort of person, usually female, usually shrill, much disliked him because of the way he looked and sounded. He rode with the punches and accepted his appearance, visual and verbal, as a sort of camouflage, which had the effect of concealing his true self from friend and foe alike. This was just as well, not least because Bognor, perversely, preferred the company of his natural enemies. His friends couldn't begin to understand this, and Bognor reciprocated.

His was a small department. In the old days, Parkinson had been the crusty old boss and he the thrusting Young Turk. Well, up to a point. Even Bognor saw the humorousness of the idea of him as thrusting young anything. Parkinson was long since retired and dead into the bargain, though the ultimate demise had been quite recent. After the old boy had spent a decently long retirement, he finally died in the fullness of years at home in his slippers. Not a bad way to go: Scotch in hand, together with a half-complete *Times* crossword.

Now, it was he who had become the crusty old boss and Contractor the thrusting Young Turk. There was no one else of serious substance. SIDBOT had always been a girl of slender means; a lean outfit; a small streamlined organization which habitually punched above its weight. This irritated smarter, bigger departments, which often found themselves out-thought and outmanoeuvred.

He sighed and felt briefly smug. The sense of self-satisfaction did not persist, alas, for he felt too much like a good deed in a naughty world, and he firmly believed that, while his was a model department, this meant that there were many other departments which were pretty grim. Life itself was pretty grim, but maybe that was another matter. He took a Hobbesian view of human existence, even though he personally had rather enjoyed what he was increasingly aware had to be thought of in the past tense. He was often asked to accept that his meaningful life was over, and even though he contested this view robustly, he was forced to recognize that there was some truth in it. Retirement was looming; he had collected his bus pass; he was soon to be a pensioner. But that didn't mean he had given up, even if he was forced to accept that he was now an old man in a hurry.

Plenty of time, though, for some final flourishes, and now that he had got his gong, now that he was running an office, he felt unshackled. He still had time for dishing out surprises and even producing some bloody noses. This he enjoyed, and in young Contractor, he believed he had a willing and able accomplice.

'Anything else, boss?' his subordinate asked.

Bognor said there wasn't anything else. Contractor hadn't finished though. 'From where I sit, it looks as if the vicar killed himself,' he said. 'Anyway, you'll never prove anything else. If I were you, I'd enjoy the show. They say Allgood talks a better book than he writes. Which wouldn't be difficult.'

'I've heard that too,' said Bognor. 'In fact, I'm seeing him again any minute. I missed his session this morning. Talking to the widow, instead. Heavy going.'

'Tough shit,' said Contractor with a definite note of irony. Talking to widows was part of the job. It went with the territory. If you didn't like it, then you should shuffle papers around like most civil servants in Whitehall.

'I'll look forward to your call,' said Bognor, more or less meaning it. He put the phone down. He supposed he should use his mobile more and master texting. However, he didn't care for the contraption and had been brought up to believe that a man should always be master of his machines. He was afraid that mobiles were gaining the upper hand, which was why he stuck to old-fashioned landlines wherever possible. He believed, probably wrongly, that where they were concerned, he was in charge.

He hated mobiles almost as much as he hated laptops but needs must. He told very few people his mobile number and even pretended to various interested parties that he disbelieved in them so bitterly that he did not own one. He liked the sort of telephone you wound up. His idea of a proper number was single figures and an exchange with letters like Juniper or Flaxman. He had a natural aversion to numbers and was in many ways a Luddite. He hankered after ink and a fountain pen even if he drew the line at a quill.

Now that he was nearing retirement, he worried more and more about the verdict of others, and especially of the Almighty and his minions. Because of his new 'K' and his position as boss of SIDBOT, he would qualify for obituaries in papers of what used to be called 'record'. *The Times*, for instance. He did not wish to be the victim of simpering damnation with faint press. However, he very much suspected that he knew the identity of the principle author in that organ and he feared the worst. Never mind. He would be gone, and he doubted very much whether Murdoch papers were delivered wherever he was going. Monica would be cross though. He wanted young Contractor to write the signed piece in the *Independent*, which was his sort of thing, but the way things were going there would be no *Independent* by the time he snuffed it. It was a race to the death, and were he a betting man, he would put money on his own chances of winning this particular race. There was no handicap that he was aware of.

He didn't believe in God, nor heaven, hell or purgatory, but that didn't stop him hedging his bets with a dose of agnosticism, nor from speculating about the quality of his reception at the pearly gates. He didn't think he had much time for St Peter anyway, and definitely believed that you got a better class of person in hell. On the other hand, he had seen enough Hieronymus Bosch in Bruges to feel apprehensive about the underworld – too much toasting fork and boiling oil, and not enough reading the *Sporting Life* over a pink gin.

He had a nasty feeling that St Peter would be patronizing. 'All those talents we gave you and you ended up with a measly "K" and an insignificant office in Whitehall,' the old saint would say, shaking his head and making notes with his quill. Bognor hated being patronized, especially by those such as Saint Peter, whom he regarded as his inferiors in almost every important respect. I mean, how many GCEs did St Peter hold? Had he ever passed a driving test? Just because he was once Bishop of Rome and a martyr. No justice. Had he, Bognor, been St Peter, he'd have made a much better fist of things. Instead of which, he was going to rot in hell.

Oh, well. He wondered if the Reverend Sebastian was rotting in hell, or merely stewing gently in purgatory, before the pearly gates rolled back and he ascended some frothy white biliousness. On balance, he'd rather be down under with Groucho Marx than on cloud nine with the Reverend Sebastian. Did suicides qualify for heaven? Would the Almighty accept his findings? He doubted it.

It seemed highly probable that Allgood had been being hypothetical. Unless he had somehow been privy to a publisher's slush pile, there was no way in which he could possibly have known that the priest was keen to be printed. The sudden, mildly mysterious, death was grist to the literary lecturer's mill. A slight exaggeration, a reasonable scintilla of doubt, these were allowable ingredients if it helped him concoct a good story. There was a maxim about never letting the facts interfere with such a thing, and Bognor would lay heavy odds that Martin Allgood subscribed to it. He would, wouldn't he?

He had to accept, reluctantly, that if he were able to prove that the late vicar was murdered, he would receive no thanks. He would obviously get no thanks from the guilty party; none from the deceased or his family; nothing but opprobrium from the Fludds and others. Not for the first time, he was out on his own; on a limb which was in imminent danger of breaking and rendering him at best ridiculous, and at worst a bit of a pest. Sir Branwell and Camilla would forgive him; Monica and little Contractor would be quietly pleased. It would cut no ice with St Peter, nor the Fellows of Apocrypha College, whom he was always seeking to please. He wondered why he had chosen such an unpopular path in life. Not vocation certainly. Just human error.

He sighed again. In a quiet way, he was afraid he believed in right and wrong. His idea of tidiness was not the same as other peoples. It was the rest of the world that was out of step. That was his core belief and it sustained him. The rest of the world disagreed, but it knew, too, that they marched to a different tune.

Which was why he had to go and have further talks with little Allgood, and sort out the new loose ends the writer had exposed. He would not be thanked for it; it would lead nowhere; but it still had to be done.

TWENTY-THREE

No one liked Martin Allgood. This mattered comparatively little, since you weren't supposed to like Martin Allgood and he worked hard at making affection a matter of indifference to him. In this, he nearly always succeeded. Contractor obviously didn't care for Allgood, but he was too professional to let this interfere with his report.

Allgood had always been unpopular. In fact, it was virtually his stock-in-trade. At school he had been the school swot, pimpled with acne. School, according to the file, was a grammar school somewhere in Essex. Bognor was very bad at the geography of that county, though he shared the popular prejudice against it. He thought of the county – wrongly of course – as an urban sprawl dominated by Epping Forest, Leyton Orient Football Club and boxers training in Tudorbethan pubs, watched by criminals of a certain age in vicuña overcoats, which they didn't remove even in oppressive heat. Males from Essex did not remove their hats indoors, and once you had made a few million you smoked large Havanas, lived in a gated community and made champagne cocktails with Dom Perignon and good cognac. It did not matter that Essex was not like that, nor that Allgood was in any way typical. Essex was not Essex, and Allgood was a one-off.

After grammar school, Allgood had been to the local university where he read sociology and got a very good degree. At about this time, Allgood had his first and only book published. This was called, with a mock-genuflection in the direction of Charles Dickens and a rare modesty, *Minimal Expectations*. What about *Rubbish*? Fact or fiction? Or a mixture of both? Or a prose poem? Or a novella? No one seemed quite sure, but it had earned Allgood a place on the 'Goodbooks' list of 'Twenty-Five Best Young British

Novelists', and the undying hatred of all good men and true. The comparatively few words of *Minimal Expectations* were arguably the last Allgood wrote, or at least, the last which were issued between hard covers.

He remained, to the world at large, a writer of almost infinite promise. The tabloids hung on his every word; his opinions sought; and his views earned golden opinions and fat fees. He had a view on everything and everyone, and many people despised him for obvious reasons.

Bognor was happy to be among those who disliked the idea of Allgood, but he was the first to acknowledge that this didn't make him a murderer. He was unpleasant enough, certainly, but Bognor knew this wasn't enough in itself. Opportunity? Well, yes. Motive? Motive would have to be mildly abstract, because there was no evidence that Allgood and Sebastian had ever met. On the other hand, Allgood was an atheist, a paid-up member of the Dawkins' camp. However, he had none of Dawkins' Balliol-bred tolerance and understanding, but was on the extreme wing of the atheist tendency. He made common ground with the sort of animal lover who hated humans, and was happy to trash laboratories and kill those who worked for him. In the case of Allgood, churches were fair game and so were vicars.

He found little Allgood in the garden of the Two by Two, aka the Fludd Arms. He was smoking what would once have been called a 'gasper', and which seemed the most apposite word for the thin, self-rolled cigarette which was stuck to his lower lip. He had on corduroy bags and an open-necked shirt with a sleeveless pullover, and in front of him was a glass of vivid pink liquid, which was bubbling away like a hookah. The *on dit* was that Allgood drank. Despite the sun, which was bright, it was chilly. The author looked as if he should have been wearing a floppy bow-tie, but a tie would have interfered with his overall appearance, which was deliberately dishevelled. Almost poetic; certainly raffish. The drink should have been absinthe.

'I'm sorry I missed you,' said Bognor. 'I'm told you were very good, but duty called.'

'Sorry about that. Quite understand though. Business

before pleasure and all that rot, though I have to say that the older I get, the more I come to believe that nothing should ever get in the way of pleasure. Certainly, nothing as vulgar as business. Can I get you a tincture?'

Bognor wondered why everyone suddenly seemed to be talking funny. He felt as if he were in the Americas or Down Under. The natives spoke a form of English but it wasn't quite the same. He guessed it was not Allgood's first pink drink of the day. Nor would it be his last.

'Thank you, but no,' he said, aware that he sounded prim, as if he never touched the stuff himself. 'I won't keep you a moment.'

'Take a pew though,' said Allgood, patting the seat of the chair alongside him invitingly. It was stylish yet comfortable, made of some kind of thatch, probably worth a fortune. Bognor did as he was bade and sat.

'A young black man came up to me in the supermarket the other day . . . I practically embraced him,' said Allgood unexpectedly. Bognor did not know what to say, but looked nonplussed, which he was.

'Sorry,' said Allgood, 'Joanna Trollope talking on TV. I caught it by mistake and have been knocking it around in case I can think of something.'

'You writing something?' asked Bognor. It seemed a sensible, pleasant conversational gambit.

'Nah,' said Allgood. 'Not really. Not books. That's a mug's game.'

'What, then?' Bognor was genuinely curious. He had Allgood down as a writer of books. A novelist. 'Fiction? Fact?'

'Bit of both,' said Allgood. 'I remember years ago, a poet saying he couldn't write anything for some literary magazine because he couldn't afford to. Also, it would jeopardize his reputation as someone who had real trouble grappling with his daemons and fighting the dreaded block. If he published, he might lose his grant from the Arts Council and the local authority; might get fewer gigs. Might be regarded as, you know, commercial. He'd be thought popular. In the mainstream. Fatal. Should have realized at the time.'

'Sorry,' said Bognor, 'you've lost me.'

'I'm famous as a novelist,' explained Allgood, talking as if to a small child, 'but it's much more lucrative to do things like this.' He smiled and waved around in an expansive manner. 'Not to mention fun.'

As if on cue, Vicenza Book entered left and sat down at their table. She looked as if she had just got out of bed, smiled and nodded at Bognor, and kissed the novelist proprietorially on the lips. 'Hi, sweetie,' she said, giving every impression of being the female half of an item.

Nothing much surprised Bognor any more, but he felt obliged to say, 'I thought you had a publicist with you? Tracey or something?'

Allgood thought for a moment. 'You're right,' he said, after a while. 'She had to go back to London. Vicenza here has stepped into her breach, as it were.' He laughed. 'Haven't you, darling?'

Vicenza simpered, and Bognor had vague thoughts of killing two birds with a single stone. He was impossibly old-fashioned. Time he retired. But even so.

'You're saying you've retired from writing books?'

'You could say I've become more of a performance artist,' he said. 'Lot easier. Better paid. More kudos.'

'So, the talk this morning . . . that sort of thing is now your bread and butter.'

Allgood seemed to give this too some thought. Eventually, he said, 'Yah,' and lapsed into silence. Vicenza ordered a glass of the pink drink from a passing waiter. It was Campari and orange. Bognor, on duty, asked for a double espresso.

'But the Reverend Sebastian wanted to be a writer,' ventured Bognor. 'Ended up on the slush pile. Felt rejected. Became depressed. Took his own life as a result.'

'Did he?' asked Allgood. 'Fancy.'

'You're the one who said it. This morning. In your talk.'

'Did I?' Allgood might have been considering a completely different third party. 'How odd. Did I have any evidence?'

'I don't know,' said Bognor, feeling as if he were getting out of his depth and had no water-wings. 'Do you? Did you?'

'Pass,' he said, and then turned to Vicenza. 'What do you think, darling?'

'Dunno,' she said, 'I wasn't there. Still sleeping it off.'

She simpered, leaving no one in any doubt what she meant by 'it'. She was the 'it' girl of Mallborne, a bicycle soprano.

'Natch,' said Allgood. 'Who said I said he wrote a book?'

'Your audience,' said Bognor. 'They seemed to think you had inside knowledge.'

'Not me,' said the non-novelist. 'If I seemed to suggest such a thing, I must have been talking hypothetically. Writers these days blur the edges between fact and fiction, in speech as well as on the page. I suppose it depends what you mean by truth.'

'Yes,' said Bognor, feeling as if he were nearing home turf. The nature of truth was the sort of concept with which he was familiar. Truth, justice, right and wrong – these were the tools of his trade. His stock.

'I sometimes feel,' said Allgood, 'that if you believe something sufficiently strongly, it assumes its own truth. It may be false, but it's not because that's not what you believe. Maybe I believe the reverend wrote a book. For me, that becomes a truth, even if it's not shared. You may not accept what I say, and the Reverend Sebastian may not actually have put pen to paper. But that doesn't invalidate my belief, nor my constructing a theory around that belief, even though the theory is based on sand. It's my belief that's important, not the actuality. Do I make myself clear?'

'Not really,' said Bognor, who was groping.

'Too deep for me,' said Vicenza. 'Not that I care much.' And she laughed throatily, like one who smoked.

'It's quite simple,' said Allgood. 'All I'm saying is that truth is relative. Most people think it's an absolute, but I don't agree. Apart from anything, it's fantastically restricting. Once you accept that it's a question of degree, it opens up any number of possibilities.'

'You can't expect me to think that,' protested Bognor. 'My whole job is predicated on the basis that the world is black and white, and there is such a thing as right and wrong, guilty and innocent. I am charged with seeking out criminals and bringing them to what we call justice.'

'I'm glad you entered the caveat,' said Allgood. 'At least you appear to be capable of understanding that in real life things aren't quite as simple as they have to be in your career.'

'I question which of us is living in "real life",' said Bognor. 'Mine feels pretty real to me.'

'Touché,' said Allgood. 'Mine, likewise. Which just goes to prove the point I'm making. I'm not disparaging your reality, which is real for you; but mine is real for me too. And you should respect it.'

'Except,' said Bognor, 'when you try to proselytize. You're entitled to a skewed view of what's real, provided you keep it to yourself and don't try to inflict it on other people. You know perfectly well that your view of what happened to the Reverend Sebastian is, in our terms, a pure fabrication, but you tried to pretend that it was real in terms that my friends, your audience, understood.'

'Now you're being duplicitous,' said Allgood. 'I was arguing hypothetically, in your terms. I never pretended otherwise.'

'That's not my understanding,' said Bognor. 'Did Sebastian write a book? Did he submit it to publishers? Was it rejected?'

Allgood appeared to give this some thought, but when he came up with an answer it was as infuriating as Bognor had feared. It also took little or no account of what he had said hitherto.

'Maybe,' he said, 'maybe not.'

It was the sort of response an Apocrypha don would have produced in one of those infuriating tutorials which had nothing to do with the subject you were supposed to be studying, and everything to do with teaching you dialectic and the art of argument. Monica hated it, even though her own college had practised much the same.

'Did the vicar write a book?'

A long silence. Eventually, Allgood said, 'Not in the sense that would stand up in a court of law. I think he could perfectly well have written one, though. And if he had, he would have suffered serial rejections which would have undermined what was, by all accounts, a flimsy sense of self-confidence and self-worth. So, what I said makes perfect sense.'

'But it's a fiction,' said Bognor, angrily.

'That's what I deal in,' said Allgood evenly, 'and there is a sense in which *my* fiction is truer than *your* fact, wouldn't you agree?'

'That's not the point, as well you know.'

'Oh, but I think it is,' said Allgood. 'Life is too literal. Actually, it's a lot more interesting than plods like you make out.'

Bognor resented being described as a 'plod', but refused to rise and said nothing. He could do metaphysics but not professionally. Work was rooted in life and death, just as he believed that books should have beginnings and middles and ends, and anchovies helped out beef casseroles.

'I don't have a problem staying interested,' he said, 'and in the world I live in, a stiff is a stiff is a stiff, and it's my job to see how and why a once breathing human can have reached that sorry state. As the meerkat says "simples". It is too. And quite interesting enough, without injecting hypotheticals.'

'You would say that, wouldn't you?' said Allgood. 'It's a point of view. Not one I happen to share, but a point of view nonetheless. I respect it. I just wish you'd do the same for mine.'

Bognor was exasperated.

'I'm sorry,' he said, 'but I have a job to do. I don't have the luxury of being able to fantasize. Boring old black and white. Tiresome. Limiting. Not as good as writing a book, much less talking about it. But it's what I do. So, can you just tell me. Did the late vicar write a book? Did he submit it to one or more publishers? Was it rejected?'

'No,' said Allgood. 'Not in so many words. Not literally. Not as far as I know. It's possible but I have no proof. As you'd describe it.'

'So, you've been wasting my time?'

'I wouldn't put it like that,' said Allgood, 'but you said it.'

'I could charge you with wasting official time,' said Bognor pompously, 'but I'll let you off with a warning.'

'Thank you, I'm sure', said the novelist. 'I'd prefer to think that we look at things in a different way. You see black and white and I see grey. I believe in murk, you believe in clarity. Different.'

Bognor reflected that Allgood could be right.

'Anything I can do, just let me know,' said Vicenza Book. She looked pert and tousled.

'Likewise,' said Allgood.

They raised their glasses.

Bognor wished life was so simple. He exited left.

Perhaps life and death were naturally murky, and his efforts to make them otherwise were necessarily doomed to failure.

Pity.

TWENTY-FOUR

There was a convention involving butlers, but Bognor was damned if he could remember what it was. This may have had something to do with the diminishing number of butlers, who were a dying breed, even if one included the ersatz butlers employed by a certain sort of celebrity hotel in such places as Dubai. Or it may have had to do with Bognor's natural forgetfulness, or his belief that neither conventions nor butlers mattered much. Either the butler dunnit or he hadn't. He was either the most suspicious character or the least. Whatever, he had to be interviewed, together with his wife, who in this case, did.

These were their alibis for the time of death: Brandon was buttling and his wife doing. Sir Branwell, Lady Fludd and the Bognors themselves were there to corroborate. They may not have actually been present, but they were at the end of a bell-pull. To have nipped off to church and done the necessary would have involved a completely unacceptable risk. And the Brandons, as was the way Bognor suspected with butlers and doers, were not among the nation's risk-takers.

It was sometimes assumed that people such as the Brandons no longer existed.

Not true.

Within living memory, well almost within living memory, the Fludds of Mallborne would have employed large numbers of servants, of whom Mr and Mrs Brandon would have been the most important. Before the two socially levelling world wars, the manor would have boasted squads of lower orders, living as a sort of alternative household behind the green baize doors, much in the manner of the household made famous by the TV programme *Upstairs, Downstairs* in the 1970s. Even quite modest middle-class households would have had a couple of servants who cooked, served, drove and generally performed menial tasks for those upstairs.

People like them were the staples of golden age crime fiction, together with simpering clerics, blustering squires, long-winded lawyers, doctors who did regular 'rounds' (sometimes even on horseback) and all the other denizens of a society who knew their place and conformed to type. This world was often thought to have vanished, but it still clung on in places such as Mallborne. It was much diminished, unfashionable, unknown even to the journalists and others who sought to present a picture of contemporary life. But its fall from grace did not mean that this world had vanished. It still clung on.

Perhaps it was a vanishing age, but it was not yet gone, and the Bognors were privy to it. Or, at least, to a part of it. They knew they were lucky and that their friends, Sir Branwell and Camilla, were immensely privileged. It was incorrect, wrong, feudal, but if you were on the right side, definite fun.

The Brandons were on the wrong side of it – below the salt and on the distaff side of the green baize. This too was deceptive, for there was a real sense in which the Brandons ran the show. He was the regimental sergeant major while Sir Branwell was the ensign or second lieutenant. The baronet had breeding but was wet behind the ears; he carried a sword while RSM Brandon had only a pacing stick, silver-headed; the little officer dined in a smart mess; the sergeant-major presided over a rougher, less gilded institution. Yet, without the Brandons of this world, the army would cease to be. If Sir Branwell were abolished, no one would notice.

There was a paradox here, and its dying did not make it any less of a paradox. In a classless society, where Jack was as good as his master, there were few nuances and complexities. The old society was unfair, sometimes criminally so, but it was satisfyingly full of contradictions. One, possibly the most obvious, was that those who seemed to be in charge, were actually little more than figureheads. Jack was better than his master, but the charade was the reverse. The truth was that the true bosses were those who

seemed to be bossed, but the truth was not to be acknow-
ledged. The Sir Branwells of this world were perceived to
be the monarchs of all they surveyed, and yet the reality
was that those such as Brandon and his wife, who bowed
and curtsied, tugged at their forelocks and were kept ruth-
lessly in place, were actually the masters now, and always
had been.

'You can drop the "sir", Brandon,' said Bognor, who,
by dint of his education, his association with Sir Branwell
and, above all, his 'K', was 'officer class'. He smiled,
patronizingly. 'There are no witnesses. And I don't hold
with that sort of thing. So just relax. Call me Simon.'

'Yes, sir,' said Brandon. Then aware of Bognor's incredulous reaction, he stammered something more egalitarian,
along the lines of 'Simon . . . er . . . Mr Bognor . . . er
. . . Sir Simon.'

Bognor, not particularly a stickler for modes of address
and correct procedure, was embarrassed, and for almost the
first time, thought that perhaps his new knighthood had
merit if only when it came to ease of address. At least one
knew where one was He had never had a problem with the
head cheese at Apocrypha being constantly addressed as
'master'. There was even, he supposed, something to be
said for 'sir', if only on the grounds that it disguised
'amnesia'. He had known people who called everyone
'Sonny' or 'Darling', or even 'Fred', when they were unable
to remember someone's real name. In that sense, maybe
'sir' was no worse. It carried unfortunate undertones of
obsequiousness and deference, but it had its all-purpose
uses.

'Sorry,' said Brandon, opting out of the problem altogether
– as most people, in Bognor's anecdotal observation, usually
did. 'It's ingrained, I'm afraid. Also, I have to say that I
have a better relationship with the boss than any number of
the young, who wouldn't dream of calling anyone by
anything other than their Christian name.'

'Unless it were "mate"!' said Mrs Brandon-who-did, and
who must have been born with a forename, but seemed to
have acquired a status without one, just as governesses and

housekeepers were accorded the mythical status of 'Mrs', whether married or not.

Bognor was afraid he was becoming sidetracked and bogged down in stuff which had nothing to do with murder. Well, maybe it did. *Lese padre*. Maybe parishioners had become overfamiliar, or, on the other hand, not familiar enough. And before he could help himself, he found himself asking, 'Did you call the Reverend Sebastian, "sir"?'

This was obviously not a question either of the servants had been asked before, and it seemed to take them by surprise.

'The thing about vicars,' said Brandon eventually, and obviously speaking for both of them, 'is that he has a title and one therefore usually called him "vicar". If not, then I suppose, yes, we addressed him as "sir", but remember he was a Fludd and that made a difference.'

Bognor had forgotten that the reverend was not just a man of God, but also a Fludd, which in the local order of preference counted for rather more. He was reminded of the Cabots and their ilk in Boston, and could perfectly well understand that in the context of Mallborne and its environs, it was better to be a Fludd than a god. Presumably, a butler who worked for the senior living Fludd was superior to a mere vicar who worked for God. But he was not going down that peculiarly English path.

'Would you say you knew the vicar well?' he asked, and was rewarded once again by the appearance of original thought. This was gratifying, almost as if he had asked an original question.

'Difficult to say, sir,' answered Brandon after a silence. 'You see he was our vicar.'

'Quite,' said Bognor. 'I mean, absolutely.'

There was a pause. Awkward.

Bognor broke it.

'Would you say you and Mrs Brandon were churchgoers? C of E? Know what I mean?'

'The missus and I are Methodists,' said Brandon, 'born and bred. But, of course, there's no Methodist Church in Mallborne, and once we entered service with Sir Branwell's father, God bless the colonel, we sort of became C of E like everyone else.'

'I quite understand,' said Bognor. He did too. The Church of England was that sort of religion. A matter of social convenience, as much as a true church with one foundation. If it had a foundation, it had more to do with what sort of newspaper one read, how one voted, and whether one dressed up to attend, than with true religion. True religion in the C of E was in short supply, and many who adhered to it, believed it was better that way.

'So, basically, you saw the Reverend Sebastian once a week in church?'

'And when he and Mrs Fludd came for sherry.'

This was Mrs Brandon. She had spoken. Bognor had the definite impression that while her husband did most of the talking, it was she who did most of the thinking.

'Did they often come for sherry?'

'Usually after matins. Mainly on high days and holy days.' This was Brandon, back in his accustomed speaking role.

'So, you really only saw the vicar in his official capacity?'

'I suppose so. You could say that the sherry was semi-official. But it was duty sherry. Not a lot of fun.'

The Brandons managed a wintry smile.

'And Mrs Fludd? The rector's wife.'

'She sang in the choir,' said Brandon. 'Soprano. Not very good. We called her the red-faced warbler. Not as good as she thought she was. She thought she was quite special. Led to even more friction with the barmaid's daughter. She's here this year, calling herself Vicenza Book. Not what we called her when she lived here. But she can sing, I'll give her that. Mrs Brandon and I know a bit about singing. Got all the Tenors on DVD, and Bryn Terfel. She was good. Mrs Fludd wasn't. Not her fault.'

He stopped suddenly. He had obviously said too much. Or thought he had.

'So your relations with the deceased and his wife were formal, correct, but slightly distant.'

The Brandons thought for a moment.

'Yes,' agreed Brandon, speaking as usual, for both. 'You

could say that. Nothing against the gentleman. Nor Mrs Fludd. But we weren't what you'd call, intimate.'

'I see,' said Bognor, thinking that people like the Brandons were the wise monkeys of the situation. They saw loads; heard a great deal; talked among themselves. But they were not part of the action. Dispassionate observers. Well, uninvolved observers. Worth plugging into, but not themselves, of the party, and therefore above – or below – suspicion.

'Any theories?' he asked, with assumed casualness.

Brandon seemed startled, as if he had been asked something improper, as indeed he had.

'Certainly not,' he said, seeming affronted and managing to convey the idea that it was a question that should never have been asked, much less answered.

Bognor felt quelled.

'I just wondered,' he said, blustering, 'if you had any theories about how the vicar met his end. I understand that you two know an awful lot about what goes on in Mallborne and I just wondered whether—'

The butler cut in.

'Will that be all, sir?' he asked, just as generation upon generation of his ancestors must have asked people such as himself. It was not a question at all, being more of a rebuke. It was a reminder, above all, that while things might appear to change, they didn't, in reality, change nearly as much as some people would have you believe. A certain sort of person knew as much, or more, as anyone; a certain sort of person knew his place, but his apparent place belied reality; a certain sort of person was in charge. Such a person now stood before him, and behind him stood the inevitable wife who, as always, in, what Bognor was increasingly inclined to accept was the battle of the sexes, wore the trousers.

He felt suitably small and much reduced; but he knew his place. The Brandons knew theirs too, and, in this instance, they were, like it or not, above the fray. And they were keeping their counsel, no matter who asked them to say what they knew.

It was ever thus.

Difficult, unfashionable, but true.

He had a call from Harvey Contractor in indecently quick time. Harvey was always in indecently quick time. He was also precise and accurate, and did as he was asked, plus some. Bognor was lucky to have him. The Board of Trade, even more so.

He was laughing when he came on line.

'I'm calling from Kew,' he said. 'On a bench by the lake. Cold but bright, and I've found what you wanted.'

'Which was?'

Bognor had not forgotten, but he wanted Contractor to repeat the info. Kept him on his toes, though this was seldom necessary. Others might rock back on their heels, but not Harvey Contractor.

'I checked out the army list, and particularly had a look at the 13th Mobile in the 1950s,' said Contractor. 'Our friend the brigadier was there all right. And, as I suspected, but you didn't quite spell out, there was a padre doing his national service at the same time by the name of Sebastian Fludd. Also a chap who sounds like a promoted sergeant major by the name of Brandon. Isn't the Fludds' butler called Brandon?'

'Yes,' said Bognor.

This he had not been expecting.

'Not right for him,' he said, 'but an odd coincidence. Quite a usual name but not that usual. Not our man though.'

'Could be his dad,' said Contractor. 'Was Brandon an army brat?'

'Could well have been.' His boss was thinking on his feet. This was tiresome but sometimes needs must. This was one of those occasions. The trick was not to let anyone else know.

'I've already spoken to the brigadier but I didn't know about the national service padre. Would you mind having a word? In person. He's London based.'

'Already have,' said Contractor. 'Cup of tea at his home. Knightsbridge or thereabouts.'

This was maddening but typical. One of many reasons why they enjoyed a love-hate relationship. It was horribly predictable of Contractor to be ahead of the game and to have anticipated his boss's desire. What's more, Contractor would wheedle stuff out of the brigadier that would have eluded Bognor. Contractor had a habit of going for the jugular in the nicest possible way. That was progress. Contractor was not as nice as he looked; Bognor nicer.

'Ah,' said Bognor.

'Did I do right, boss?' he asked.

'Of course you did right,' said Bognor snappily. 'You always do. It would just be nice if, for once, you waited to be asked.'

'Sorry, boss.'

'Don't pretend.' Bognor was reminded of the time that Leslie Compton, a footballing hero from Arsenal days had disregarded his captain's command, had scored a famous winning goal, and had apologized to the skipper for disobeying orders. He hadn't meant it any more than Contractor.

'You OK?' Contractor wanted to know. Bognor was touched, although he recognized that the concern was at least partly selfish. Bognor's absence left his minion dangerously exposed to marauding mandarins from elsewhere in Whitehall. Bognor, by dint of years, if nothing else, had clout. Other men and women were frightened of him. He never thought it would happen, and put it down partly to age, and partly to a certain recklessness which came with longevity. On his way up the ladder, he cared about life and about the impression he was making on others. Now that he had gone as high as he was going, he no longer gave a stuff. He simply couldn't care less. Other people knew this. And were afraid.

'I'm fine. You?'

'We miss you,' said Contractor, and part of him may even have meant it. He had grown quite fond of the old thing. Self-interest was there too. Bognor was a grouchy old guard dog, but once he was out on his rounds, the rest of the world came sniffing around, pulling rank and peeing on the shoots of independence and unorthodoxy. Contractor was keen on both, and clever enough, particularly when protected by Bognor, to get away with it. Without the protective bark of Bognor, however, he was vulnerable.

'Don't let the buggers get you down,' said Bognor, only too aware of the crippling orthodoxy of the men who ran other departments. He knew that they would be trying to pull rank in his absence; attempting to get Contractor to toe the line behind which they liked to hunker down.

Smooth, suave and second-rate. Cowards certainly, but bullies too. At least, when they could get away with it. In the nicest possible way. It was what foreigners so disliked about a certain sort of old-fashioned Brit. You couldn't trust them, but they were such gents. Dressed properly, as well.

'Don't worry,' he said, 'I can look after myself. Be nice to have you back though.'

Bognor frowned. He was supposed to be on holiday. He doubted whether Contractor really could look after himself. It would be good to be back. He snapped shut the mobile.

In for a penny, he thought, and punched in another number.

'Pathology,' said a voice, and he asked for the man to whom he had been so rude.

'Sorry if I seemed . . . er . . . well . . . sorry,' he said.

The voice at the other end sounded conciliatory and used to apologies such as this.

'It's all right,' said the voice. It obviously wasn't but Bognor let it pass.

'I just wonder,' said Bognor, 'in the case of the late Vicar of St Teath's, Mallborne, whether it would have been possible for the deceased to tie a rope round a rafter, put it round his neck, step on to a stool and then kick it from beneath him. If it were suicide, then that's what he would have had to do. Does your examination provide hard and fast answers?'

All this prolonged and original thought was good for Bognor's ego, and he could hear the forensic scientist cudgelling his grey matter at the other end of the line for several gratifying seconds. Eventually, the pathologist spoke.

'It's a grey area,' he said. 'Routine DNA testing showed evidence of the widow's presence. There were a number of other traces. Churches are busy places, after all. The rope had been handled by several different people. So, it's perfectly possible that one or more other people were involved. Technically speaking, it would have been possible for the deceased to have carried out the entire operation single-handed, but my own guess is that it would have been unlikely, given that he was not a naturally strong or athletic person.'

'No,' said Bognor, 'I agree. And while DNA testing makes it possible to say who had been in the church and who had touched the rope, would it also be possible to eliminate other people who hadn't either been in the building, or handled, what for want of a better word, one has to think of as the murder weapon?'

There was another gratifying, cogitating silence.

'Difficult to say,' said the expert. 'It's a grey area.'

'Quite.'

He wanted to say that forensics was too often a grey area; that post-mortem examinations only told you what you already knew; and that detection was best left to detectives. The ambiguity of the autopsy to alliterate. However, he thought better of all this and merely, meekly, thanked the pathologist for his time and trouble, closed the nasty little machine, consulted his watch and realized that he had missed lunch. Even so, he needed to discuss progress with Monica. Monica was the only person, apart from the absent Contractor, on whom he could really rely.

He met her in the drive up to the manor. She was looking smug and humming. Always a bad sign. Especially when, as now, she was humming Mozart.

'I skived off,' she said. 'Made my excuses and left. I've just been having an absolutely delicious beef sandwich at the Two by Two. Underdone beef, brown bread, fresh butter, home-made English mustard. And a glass of jolly-nice Rioja, made in an obscure village by an old man called Pablo.'

'As one is,' said Bognor, unamused. His tummy rumbled.

'Not a trace of snail; not a hint of porridge,' said his wife, not noticing. 'Perfection. Just what the doctor ordered. Pub

food as she was intended. The best of British. And Gunther
came by for a chat and let me into a juicy little secret.'

There was a bench nearby, dedicated to Mavis, with dates.
They sat on it. The sun shone, lemony, thin and antiseptic,
bright enough but conveying no warmth.

'Secret?' said Bognor, envying the sandwich and the glass
of wine but not saying so. He thought of the Rubáiyát and
fancied himself briefly as Omar Khayaam, curbing this flight
of fancy, as speedily as it had arisen.

'He didn't like the vicar. Hated him, in fact. I think it
was mutual. The Reverend Sebastian didn't like poofters.'

'Plenty of gay people around. Even in Mallborne. That's
no excuse for a serious feud.'

'They fell out over food. Gunther being gay didn't make
things easier.'

'Everyone in Mallborne fell out over food with Gunther.
He'd be all very well in Bray. Or even Padstow. But Mallborne
is another matter. They don't go for his sort of scoff. It's
classic meat and two veg country.'

'I know, I know.' Monica knew. 'The point is that it could
be a motive. Gunther thinks so anyway. There was a grudge
which persisted; business was unfinished. Worst of all there
was a campaign on some allegedly impartial website. Lots
of anonymous people claimed to have eaten at the Two by
Two and hated it. Some even alleged food poisoning.
Gunther thinks the vicar was behind it. He's afraid it could
be a strong enough motive to excite suspicion.'

Once again, Bognor exercised his scepticism. 'He would
say that. Might even think it. But at the end of the day, it's
like I say – we've only got his word for it.'

'Well,' she said, 'he's a worried man.'

'Which,' said her husband, 'may explain the uncharacteristically orthodox beef sandwich. He saw you coming.'

His tummy rumbled agreement, but once more Monica
affected not to notice.

TWENTY-FIVE

He kept thinking about the unexpected beef sandwich and glass of red wine, but had to make do with builder's tea and biscuits. He rather liked basic tea with sugar and milk, and Branwell and Camilla provided Chocolate Olivers, which were, arguably, the best biscuits ever invented. For a man who had missed lunch, he was therefore reasonably happy.

Mallborne should, by rights, have been the cosiest place imaginable; its vicar the least likely corpse. He was reminded of the old Conan Doyle adage about the smiling English countryside being far more lethal and threatening than the mean streets of the most sinister city. Lincolnshire was more menacing than London; Gloucestershire than Glasgow; Sussex than Stoke.

It was fashionable to suggest otherwise. Chicago, Los Angeles and Detroit had meaner streets than anything funny old Britain had to offer, and latterly it was Danes and Icelanders who had acquired a reputation for really revolting killings. Scandinavians did sex; Americans assassination; the English nothing more deadly than scones with cream and strawberry jam.

And yet.

Horrible things happened in the English countryside. Harmless spinsters and blameless bachelors in picture-postcard English villages dropped dead in mysterious and often rather disgusting circumstances. Honeysuckle and roses under a roof of thatch afforded a plausible disguise, just as, let's face it, so did much of the apparatus of the typical English village. A benign exterior often concealed something nasty. Things were just as likely to go bump in the night when you could see the Milky Way, as when the only lights were neon; the woodshed concealed as much nastiness as any tenement; and the nightshade in the environmentally friendly hedgerow was as deadly as the detritus in the gutter. Cosiness was an illusion; security a sham; there might well be honey still for tea, but only a supremely gullible innocent would accept it from a stranger.

Bognor knew all this in theory, but it didn't make it any easier to accept when it hit him in the face. He really had thought that a few days with his old university friend and his wife in the sleepy town of the Fludds would be a happy, peaceful holiday. A literary festival, even allowing for the scratchy reputation of rival writers, was almost by definition, a somnolent affair. He had anticipated a lazy holiday, far from madding crowds and sudden death.

And now this.

'Almost everyone in the place seems to have had a motive for killing the vicar,' he said conversationally, chomping on a delicious biscuit.

'Oh, come on, Simon,' said Camilla, pouring strong black tea from an enormous silver teapot. 'Present company excepted.'

This was Bognor's belief but it was an exaggeration, and though acceptable, perhaps, as a figure of speech, it would not show up in any written report to which he attached his name. He was much too canny for that. What he really meant was that the Reverend Sebastian was the sort of person who was probably better off dead. What he also meant, but naturally failed to say, was that if he were the murdering kind, then he would cheerfully have murdered the Reverend Sebastian Fludd. Bognor, basically, believed that the world would be a better place without clergymen. At least, he believed that the good cleric was someone who had at least one, and preferably several, lay lives before being ordained. He also believed that successful clergymen smoked, drank, swore and probably gambled. If they did, the last they often lost. But then Bognor liked sinners and he liked losers. The dead vicar was definitely one of life's losers, but he certainly wasn't a sinner either. And Bognor believed that sanctimonious souls were better off dead, and that most people wished them to be so. If necessary, most people would help them on their way. Or would if they did not run a real risk of being caught.

'Oh, all right,' said Bognor. 'But there are a surprising number of people who will be only too happy to see the back of the vicar.'

'That says something about the nature of belief in today's society,' said Sir Branwell, drinking tea with enthusiasm. 'Dawkins and his friends have a lot to answer for. One of the things I always liked about religion in the good old days was its non-aggressive character. It just was. No one particularly believed in stuff like transubstantiation or the virgin birth, or what have you. Never gave it much thought, if they were honest. Just formed up in their best suits on Sunday, belted out something familiar from *Hymns Ancient and Modern* and buggered off home until the next week's show. It was like glue or cement. Kept everyone in their place but everyone knew where that was. Made a good noise, gave a lot of comfort. Good thing, very.'

'Talking of *Hymns Ancient and Modern*,' said Bognor, addressing his wife, 'did you get anywhere with the hymn board.'

''Fraid not,' said Monica shaking her head. 'There's something there, all right, but I haven't worked out what it is. Not yet, anyway. But I will. Promise.'

She would too. If Monica promised something, she would deliver. That's what promises were about. As far as she was concerned. She was that old-fashioned figure – a woman of her word.

'Anyhow,' said Bognor, helping himself, unasked, to another biscuit. I'm afraid I seem to have uncovered something of a can of worms in this little paradise. Everyone loathed the vicar.'

This was not an absolute truth, more of a conversational ploy. In a community such as Mallborne, most people were indifferent to the vicar. He was a fact of life, much like the squire or the doctor. Most people didn't loathe the vicar, because they couldn't be bothered. Bognor, living in London, didn't even know who his vicar was. Had he done so, he felt he should loathe him, but he was a kind-hearted person and also disinclined to do the right thing. This meant that he tended to rather like priests. On the other hand, he took little satisfaction in this. In fact, he regarded it as a lapse.

'Not us,' protested Camilla. 'We thought he was a perfectly nice little man. And his wife. Charming.'

'If you like that sort of thing,' said Sir Branwell. He spoke stiffly, as one who patently did not like that sort of thing, but considered himself (wrongly) too well-bred to show it.

'You have a perfectly acceptable alibi, and I don't for a second believe you killed him. However, that's not the same as saying you liked him. Or the Reverend Mrs. You tolerated them. They kept the vicarage warm; they ran the church and everything that went with it. But that's not the same as liking them.'

'Vicars are trade,' said Sir Branwell. 'Simple as that. They are. They exist. They help keep things in their place. But their place is, well, put it this way, Sebastian and Dorcas were not one of us.'

'Well,' said Camilla, 'they used the front door.'

'In a manner of speaking,' said her husband, 'but they weren't the sort of people you'd have to dinner. Not for pleasure. Duty, perhaps. But that's something else altogether.'

Sir Branwell was not Lord Lieutenant for nothing. He knew the Queen and she had been to stay. Actually, he thought the Windsors and especially Prince Philip were foreign upstarts, but this was an opinion he did not often voice out loud. Nor did he know any of the royal family at all well. In fact, they wouldn't know him from the proverbial bar of soap if they met outside the county. Within it, however, he was Her Majesty's Lord Lieutenant and, in a very real sense, monarch of all that he surveyed.

'Men of God,' he said, 'are a necessity. However, the necessity is painful. And that includes the bishop.'

'I think Ebenezer is rather a good egg,' protested Bognor. 'He's by way of being a bit of a friend.'

'You have to have bishops and vicars, but I take a Cromwellian view of such people. If you catch my drift.'

The Bognors caught it but were not altogether impressed. They knew that Branwell was a cheerful agnostic, who took a pragmatic view of clerics and the church. Broadly speaking, he liked the noise, but expected 'his' chaps to toe the line, not step over it, or rock the boat. They were part of a team dedicated to decency, common sense and, above all, the preservation of the status quo. The last thing he wanted creeping into their behaviour, was any sort of damned religious nonsense. As far as he was concerned, the true Christ was a dangerous lefty and would have been run out of town, double quick. Probably wore sandals and read the *Guardian*. On the other hand, Branwell was not stupid, nor ill-educated. When he spoke of Cromwell, he might just as well have been talking of Thomas as Oliver. He had read Hilary Mantel, but did not believe hers was a historically accurate account of a flawed life.

Sir Branwell was right wing but that did not make him a patsy.

'Point taken,' said Bognor. 'You regarded the Fludds as socially inferior and professionally suspect, but you were in charge and you tolerated them. Above all, you didn't kill him. End of story. Correct?'

'In a nutshell,' agreed Branwell. 'Next?'

'Gunther,' said Bognor. 'He and the Reverend Sebastian had a falling out over the harvest dinner. Gunther suspects that Sebastian conducted a vendetta against him on one or more Internet sites like TripAdvisor. But Gunther has a reasonable alibi and, for the record, I don't think he killed the vicar either.'

'He's an emet,' said Camilla. 'He comes from Essex or somewhere.'

'Germany even.' Sir Branwell laughed. 'Whatever else he is, Gunther's certainly no Kraut. With respect. So, Germany's a joke. Besides, Germany doesn't do haute cuisine.'

'Don't you like Gunther, either?'

'Oh,' said, Branwell, 'he's all right, if you like that sort of thing. He paid perfectly decent money for the Arms, and he can't help being the sort of bloke who helps out at tea parties. Not that I have anything against shirt-lifters. Or ersatz Krauts, come to that. On the other hand, there's a time and a place for everything, and I just don't happen to think we're ready for young Battenburg yet. Maybe in a generation or two, but right now, I'd say we were into heterosexual Brits who produce decent pub grub. I'll bet you anything you like that young Gunter will be gone in a year or two. Like I said, I've absolutely nothing against the chap, but at the end of the day he's only the cook. I mean, I'm perfectly fond of Mrs Brandon, but that doesn't mean to say that I think she's anything other than a perfectly nice artisan. She does exactly what she's paid to do, no more, no less. Doesn't give herself airs and graces. Doesn't pretend to be anything more than she is. Salt of the earth.'

It was on the tip of his tongue for Bognor to observe that the salt of the earth was Mrs Brandon's glass ceiling, but he thought better of it. Better leave any fancy wordplay to his host.

'Do you think the Reverend Sebastian was writing hostile web reports in an effort to get rid of Battenburg?'

'If he was, he wasn't the only one,' said Branwell. 'Lots of the town were at it. Quite a creative enterprise. I like snails and I like porridge, but, as far as I'm concerned, never the twain shall meet. The one thing we don't want is a whole posse of foreign foodies mincing down to Mallborne, and hanging out at the pub taking pictures of each other and various kinds of foam with their Instamatics. That's all very well for that American with the funny voice.'

'You mean Lloyd Grossman,' said Monica, not from her tone of voice, agreeing with a word he said. 'He left ages ago. *Masterchef* is presented by an Australian and a London greengrocer. Grossman does mass-produced sauce.'

'Just another cook as far as I'm concerned,' said Fludd. 'Like I said, I've nothing whatever against cooks, and nothing whatever against food. I just think they should know their place. And if the vicar agreed with me, then that's one thing on which we saw eye to eye.'

'Eye for a tooth,' said Bognor, facetiously and regretted it.

'As in nature red . . .' said his host, thinking himself pretty clever.

'Anyway the cook didn't do it,' said Bognor. 'Flawless alibi and not his style, anyway. I don't see him killing anything, even if it was edible. So you can rule him out.'

'Mind you, I would put the bit of high-class cannibalism past him. Sort of thing you'd expect from Essex man.'

Bognor judged it best to change the subject.

'Vicenza Book,' he said. 'What about the sultry soprano?'

'The town bicycle,' said the squire. 'Slept with practically every red-blooded single male in town, and more besides, if you'll pardon my French, ladies. Vicar wasn't entirely sensible when it came to her and her mum, and I dare say she harboured a grudge, but she's never looked back since leaving us. She has as good an alibi as anyone else, and I'd say no. Why? I mean, I know why, but . . .'

Bognor wondered whether Sir Branwell had bedded either mother or daughter. Probably on the family billiard table. He wouldn't put it past him. And yet.

If Vicenza Book had not existed, then Laurie Lee would have invented her. She was a hoyden with décolletage and a heart of gold, though, despite the large and much exposed mammaries, she had vital organs of ice or steel, depending on one's point of view. What you saw, was most definitely not what you got, though she had always sung like the proverbial angel. Even in the bath.

Her real name was Marigold Bean, though she hated the name Marigold and called herself Mary in her early teens. She took the name Vicenza Book as soon as she turned professional. She chose Vicenza because she wanted something Italian, and dabbed with a pair of compasses. She selected Book because she wouldn't be seen dead with one; had never even attempted to read one. Bognor reflected that everyone, these days, abandoned their given names and opted for a new one. He personally never cared for Bognor, with which he had been born, nor for Simon, which he had been given because his mother liked the noise it made. As for his second name, Montmorency, the less said the better. But he never considered changing any of them. Chaps didn't.

The Reverend Sebastian hated the Beans. Of course he did. He was an ascetic authentic man of the cloth, and he therefore hated strong drink, joking, jesting and excessive behaviour. He forgave, naturally, because that was what our Lord ordered, but he didn't like it. He was a natural do nothing, a creature of minimalism. He was thin, pale and not very interesting. Enjoyment did not come naturally. In fact, it didn't come at all.

The reverse was true of Marigold or Mary Bean. She lived for enjoyment and without it she was nothing. She liked to shout, she liked to swear, and she enjoyed sex.

When the vicar came calling and her mother was out, something was bound to happen. And if it didn't happen, it was alleged to have done so. It was, on the other hand, unprovable and grey. In such circumstances, it always was. There were no witnesses and two sexes. The eternal nightmare.

It was one reason for his abiding unease over crimes of rape. This had led to sometimes enraged and abusive arguments with Monica, not because he was a male chauvinist pig or believed that women made false sexual accusations. Actually, he rather prided himself on his credentials as a new man, and thought of himself as a bit of a women's libber. He just had a tendency for thinking things grey, for seeing all sides of every question and, above all, having what he believed was a nice regard for the fair play principle. Monica, on the other hand, was much more black and white, and only believed in fair play when it suited her. That, though, he conceded, typically, was only his point of view. Monica thought otherwise.

Anyway, the point was that something had obviously happened. Mary Bean, nubile, flirty and unashamedly female, was alone in the house when the Reverend Sebastian came calling. He was etiolated, puritan, off-white, but in his own, possibly frustrated way, as male as she was, more obviously, female. Had he made a pass? Had she baited him? Was it a real misunderstanding or a product of wishful thinking?

Bognor shrugged. It didn't much matter and one would never know the exact truth, anyway. Contractor didn't know, either. It obviously did not interfere with Sebastian's assessment of la Whatsit's musical ability. He had evidently been very supportive of Vicenza's visit to the festival and as convinced of her musical ability as everyone else. Vicenza's voice was unquestionably brilliant. She occasionally did the Katherine Jenkins-Hayley Westenrath thing and stooped to singing the Italian national anthem before rugby matches, though it had to be admitted that the Italian national anthem was worth singing, even if the team wasn't worth supporting. Vicenza seemed to have a soft spot for rugby players, though it had to be conceded that her spot was soft for most males, and she would probably have bedded even Berlusconi, particularly if the money had been right. She would probably have demanded a portfolio, but the prime minister clearly gave them out to his girlfriends like so much confetti.

Sebastian had a fine collection of old 78s and enjoyed Mahler. He was something of an all-round opera buff. Something, ill-defined, told Bognor that the reverend also fancied Vicenza carnally. He couldn't say what this was, and there was nothing in Contractor's report to suggest such an aberration. Perhaps it was just a hunch. His hunches tended to play well, though he was the first to concede that they were, in the end, only hunches. The Reverend Sebastian may have seemed anaemic, but there had been more flesh and blood to him than anyone else cared to admit. And Vicenza Book was *all* flesh and blood. If she had done national service, she would have been described as 'over-sexed' and given bromide in her tea.

The phone trilled and Lady Fludd answered. Bognor realized, as she told the caller that he was at her elbow, that he had, as usual, switched off his mobile. It was bound to be Contractor, and he was bound to berate the boss for rendering himself inaccessible, or at least overheard.

'Bognor,' said Bognor into the phone, which was black and traditional, and very much to his taste.

It was indeed Contractor.

'I thought you'd like to know, boss,' he said, 'that the Brandon was a promoted sergeant major and had a son who went into service. Also, and I think this could be important, there was a famous debagging. Our friend, the deceased, left soon afterwards, but it left a nasty smell. Hushed up, of course. Still known in Mobile circles as the Blenkinsop black balls-up. Our friend has never talked about it outside the mess since it happened, but, if you ask me, he seemed rather pleased with the memory. Not altogether unhappy to have been rumbled. But that doesn't make him a murderer.'

'No,' said Bognor, 'I'm afraid not.'

TWENTY-SIX

The demolition of Brigadier and Mrs Blenkinsop was over in short order. The motive was new; the alibi always on the flimsy side; but the intrinsic probability limited. This was, admittedly, down to intuition and would not hold water in court. Over the years, however, it had stood Bognor in good stead. He simply did not see the Blenkinsops as a ruthless killing machine. It also seemed significant that there was no sign of opposition. Whether or not the vicar had departed entirely of his own volition was still a matter of conjecture. There was no sign of a fight. And, in Bognor's opinion at least, the vicar would have fought the brigadier and his wife.

'I absolutely agree,' said Camilla, 'that you have produced a number of people who disliked vicars in general and this one in particular. But most of them live outside the town. I think you'll find the average Mallburnian remarkably tolerant. The philosophy here has always been "live and let live". Even if the locals shared the average metropolitan dislike of poor little Sebastian, I don't think they wished him any particular harm. Only seriously zealous and peculiar people listen to sermons, or pay any attention to what the padre says. Anglicanism is a minority business. You'll find much more passion in Southall or Bradford. Muslims and Sikhs take religion pretty seriously. You could say that even Jews and Catholics are the same. The C of E has always been a great deal more restrained. And nowhere more so, dare I say it, than in Mallborne.'

'And she speaks as an outsider herself.'

This, in a manner of speaking, was true. Camilla's father had been an academic at the University of Edinburgh. She came, if she came from anywhere, from the Kingdom of Fife. She was not a Mallburnian; not even English.

'And Allgood certainly isn't from these parts,' said Bognor, moving on to the next most serious suspect.

'Probably from the same part of Essex as the cook,' said Fludd.

'What have you got against Essex?' asked Monica. 'Parts of it are perfectly nice, and some quite acceptable people come from there: Constable, Paul Jennings, Ruth Rendell. Some people would even include Randolph Churchill. Not me, I agree, but some would. I'd be surprised if you'd even been there.'

'Went for cricket once,' said Fludd, sharpish. 'Chelmsford. Rain. Only a couple of overs. No runs. Bailey batting.'

This was almost, but not quite, a non-sequitur.

'Whatever, Allgood seems to have made everything up.' This was Bognor, claiming inside knowledge. After all, he had the advantage of a post-performance personal talk.

'Hmmm,' said Branwell. 'Plagiarism is a dodgy area.'

'Who said anything about plagiarism?' asked Bognor. 'My feeling about Allgood is that he's perfectly original. A plagiarist is someone who borrows from someone else.'

'Steals,' said Monica. 'A plagiarist is one who steals.'

'Novelists are always being advised to write about what they know. That means real life. And that means that writers of fiction steal their material from what actually happens. Which is why so many novels are a pale imitation of life itself. Allgood's included.'

'But you've never read an Allgood,' said Monica. 'So how could you possibly know?'

'I've read the reviews,' said Branwell, 'and I've heard him talk. That's good enough for me.'

'You surely don't believe what you read in the papers?' asked Monica, full of assumed incredulity. 'Any more than what you hear at literary festivals. It may not be plagiarized but it's certainly not the truth.'

'Whatever that is,' said her husband. He spoke morosely.

'Oh, come on, Simon,' said Sir Branwell, 'You've done a terrific job of going through the motions. You've interviewed all sorts of people with tremendous tact and circumspection, and we haven't had a jawnalist within sniffing distance. We're incredibly grateful. A real busman's holiday for you. I'm truly grateful. We all are. We can bury poor little Sebastian, let him rest in peace, draw a line in the sand and move on. Thanks, largely, to you.'

And, so, thought Bognor, that was it. He felt used, soiled, unconvinced. This was not a new feeling. Far from it. That was partly why he felt so distressed. Not for the first time, he had failed to prove what he believed. Worse than that, he had become a sort of establishment fall-guy, giving a spurious respectability to a cover-up. Perhaps he was mistaken; maybe the vicar had killed himself in this melodramatic fashion, at this inconvenient time. In any event, Bognor had been there to pour oil, to give everything an orderly respectability. In doing so, he had connived in a deception and done what authority wished.

'I always said,' said Sir Branwell, rubbing it in, 'that it was suicide. I have to say that it's gratifying to be proved right by an expert.'

'Nothing like consistency,' commented Sir Simon.

To which Sir Branwell, completely unfazed, said that he had always been taught that inconsistency was the better part of politeness, just as discretion was the better part of valour. Or words to that effect.

Bognor also winced at the use of the word 'expert'. It was not used ironically but that was its effect on him. All his life he had striven for what was right, whereas the world and his wife wanted only what was expedient. There were occasions on which Bognor felt as if he were in a macabre spaghetti western, holed up in some impregnable eyrie with only a few bullets left for his carbine and a cyanide bullet to kill himself rather than surrender. In the plain below, the enemy was the world itself – an unlikely fusion of the US Cavalry and the Apache; of Burt Lancaster, Henry Fonda and sundry bit-part actors in feathers and make-up; an impossible coalition of good and bad, in which only he was more than window dressing. His was the voice in the wilderness. Everyone else but him was out of step. He would sell his life as dearly as possible, but in the end he would bite the lethal capsule and die an unlamented and unnoticed death.

In real life, he had taken a knighthood and become head of department. He would retire gracelessly and frequent the London Library and his gentleman's club, where he would bore away at the centre table – a figure to be avoided, pitied and ridiculed. His would be a life of convention. What had once promised so much, had turned to ashes. Worse still, he was a living excuse for evil. The world was a worse place for his existence, but he gave it respectability, for he was a safe pair of hands, a man of integrity, an Apocrypha graduate.

He felt desolate and his friend was rubbing salt in his wounds.

'Just because I couldn't prove otherwise, doesn't mean that the vicar committed suicide.'

'Of course not,' said Sir Branwell. 'Cheer up and have another biscuit. Enjoy the rest of the festival. Relax.'

Upstairs in their vast, chilly bedroom Bognor flipped through the pages of his programme and told himself that he had failed.

His wife, however, seemed elated.

'I think I've cracked it,' she said. 'I was barking up completely the wrong tree. Because the clue was on a hymn board, I immediately assumed I'd find the answer in *Hymns Ancient and Modern*, whereas it was in the Bible itself. I should have known. Even the revised version of the hymnal stops in the six hundreds, so anything beginning with a seven and a nine had to come from somewhere else. QED. So the hymn board wasn't advertising hymns. It wasn't intended as a public instruction for the congregation, more of a private message. Bit like a crossword clue.'

'You've lost me,' said Bognor, 'and it doesn't matter. We record some sort of open verdict, bury the poor padre and move on. There is a line in the sand, or whatever the appropriate cliché is. Your solution is too late. Probably wrong, as well. In any case, it couldn't matter less. I've screwed up, but I've screwed up in a way that suits the Fludds and the chief constable and Dorcas and Ebenezer, and everyone else in the world. But I still have a sneaky feeling . . .'

He sighed. The refrain was frequent. Just when you had reached the peak of the mountain, you realized it was an illusion, and you had another climb to make. It was an ascent too far. He had been here before. Often.

'It was Dorcas and Ebenezer that muddled me,' said Monica. She had heard these mournful blatherings before. Many times. She had come to accept them, even to expect them. Her husband seemed not to understand that it was never too late for justice, and that in the end his wife would triumph. She always did. 'Especially Ebenezer,' continued Lady B., breezily seeming not to notice that Simon had uttered. 'I mean, there is so much in the hymnal which has to do with Ebenezer. Ton-y-botel, all that Welshness, Williams and Jones, and at least three different sets of words. As you know, the Welsh are only any good, once in a blue moon, for rugby football, singing and seaweed. Bit like the so-called Welsh language. It's just noise. Like all those pointless points in a Methodist sermon. They go on and on, the preacher is mesmerizing, but at the end of the day, you can't remember a word he said. It's just so much hot air. Same here. All red herrings of one sort or another. Nothing to do with Hymns A and M.'

'I am familiar with the tune Ebenezer.' Bognor tried to sound icy and knowledgeable, but failed at both. Still, he felt piqued, and he did know whereof he spoke. 'T.G. Williams,' he said, 'aka Thomas. 1890 to 1944. Once to every man and nation. Hail thou once despised Jesus. Not in any way to be mixed up with the often omitted line about raising "mine Ebenezer", which means "stone of help". It may have been an old folk song. Could have been washed up in a bottle. I think Williams was a plagiarist to be absolutely honest. Anyway, you're saying that the hymn is a red herring. So, what have you discovered that works?'

He was dredging up something he had been taught in Divinity at his private school many years before. It sounded good to him now, just as it did when he was little. He hoped his wife would not know enough to contradict him. But maybe it was irrelevant. Like him.

'Aha,' she said, 'I'll only tell you if you cheer up.' She

was truculent, buoyed up by her ability to find the answer and solve the conundrum. Not for nothing was she a whizz at Sudoku.

'I'm perfectly cheerful,' he lied. He always felt like this, in what should have been moments of connubial bliss. It didn't matter that he would present the solution as if it had been all his own work. He and Monica knew otherwise. They understood the truism that behind every good man, there was a woman at least as good. From time to time, Bognor pretended otherwise. Even if it were teamwork, there was a team leader and an ordinary team member, and he knew enough to understand that he was not the team leader.

'Well, all right, I'll tell you anyway. There were four hymns listed, OK?'

'OK.'

She paused, smiled, and shivered.

'Two of them were ordinary, common-or-garden real hymns. The other two are significant. The last two aren't hymns at all. They're both biblical references. One is from the first Book of Samuel and the other is from the Acts of the Apostles. One is about Ebenezer and the other is about Dorcas. Geddit?'

Bognor wasn't sure. He wasn't sure of anything any longer. His wife, however, seemed certain of all the answers and she had the bit between her teeth. He was happy to leave it to her. He had little or no alternative since, in any case, she would not allow him one.

'Carry on,' he said, lethargically, managing to imply dangerously that she was going to carry on, no matter what.

She looked at him exasperated, but was obviously too excited to care.

'One was nine-three-six. That's chapter nine of the Acts, verse thirty-six. The first of the verses telling the story of Dorcas being raised from the dead by St Peter. Except that she's really called Tabitha. Dorcas is the translation. "Now there was at Joppa a certain disciple named Tabitha, which by interpretation is called Dorcas." Those are the exact words!'

'Right,' he said, 'and the other is the passage introducing Ebenezer in the first Book of Samuel.'

'Correct,' she said, exultantly. 'Not hymns at all. Seven-one-two, if you remember. In other words, chapter seven, verse twelve, where Samuel says he's erecting a stone of remembrance to commemorate a defeat for the Philistines between Mizpah and Shen. "Samuel took a stone and set it between Mizpeh and Shen and called the name of it Ebenezer".'

'Fascinating,' said Bognor. 'So it's been staring us in the face all the time?'

'You could say that, yes.' His wife wore the expression of one who has just conquered a particularly difficult cross-word clue.

'Ebenezer and Dorcas using the hymn board for anyone quick enough and well versed enough in scripture, as it were,' said Bognor.

'So, not your average scene of crime officer,' agreed Monica. 'Nor your average pathologist. Adam Dalgleish, perhaps. Or Peter Wimsey. But not in real life.'

'Your "average pathologist" wouldn't have visited the scene of crime,' said Bognor, a shade pedantically. 'It's one reason I'm so sceptical about pathology, autopsies and post-mortem examinations. They've never yet told me anything I didn't know already, and often significantly less as of now. I knew I didn't like the pathologist. Solving the clues of the hymn board needed someone like you. Like us.'

His wife smirked and said nothing. There was no need.

Dorcas was drinking Bovril when Bognor arrived. He had a feeling that Dorcas was always drinking Bovril, and in a metaphorical sense he was, perhaps, right. The Bovril was in a blue and white mug of a hooped design known as Cornish, and it was scaldingly hot. Dorcas's ancestors would have drunk Bovril too, but they would have called it 'Beef tea'.

She did not offer Bognor anything, but asked him if he would like to sit, which he did.

For a while, he remained silent, his gaze held by a sampler, early Victorian, framed on the wall opposite.

She sat too and sipped Bovril. She too did not speak.

In the hall, a grandmother clock ticked noisily and struck a quarter past, whirring before it did so.

'Sebastian wasn't dead when you entered the church,' he said. It was a statement, not a question. He was not expecting an answer, let alone a 'no'.

She bent her head.

'You cracked the code.'

Same thing. A statement. Not a question.

'We cracked the code. I cracked the code. Not difficult. Particularly not when one realized one wasn't dealing with hymns but the Bible.' He was being shameless. Left to his own devices he would almost certainly have been none the wiser. Without Monica, he would have assumed that all four sets of numbers referred to hymns.

'The Bible?'

She needed to know that his deduction was based on legwork and knowledge, not fluke.

'Yes.' he said. He was being economical with the truth, and they both knew it.

The silence should have been awkward but instead it seemed oddly companionable.

Presently, the vicar's widow said, 'It was Ebenezer's idea.'

'Ebenezer's?'

'Yes.' After a while, she added, by way of explanation, 'He wanted it to be easy but not too easy. He was anxious that our presence should be known but not to everyone. He seemed to think that the information should be privileged. Given only to people who were privy to a little knowledge and had at least an elementary grasp of deductive principles.'

'I see,' said Bognor. He didn't but it did not seem to matter. He thought it meant that Ebenezer wanted them to know but not the world and his wife. It was the work of an elitist.

'Poor Sebastian,' she said. 'He'd given up really. Everything was suddenly too much.'

'Really? Most people thought he was pretty much on top of things. He was intending to deliver his sermon, after all.

That doesn't sound like someone who's given up.' Bognor was bothered by this. The dead vicar did not give the posthumous impression that he thought that day would be his last. He was preparing his sermon. That meant that he hoped to deliver it.

'Maybe only those who knew him intimately quite realized. He was surprisingly good at keeping up appearances. That mattered right to the end. He didn't want anyone to know that he was exhausted. I sometimes think, late at night, that it was other people's opinions that killed him. They mattered far more than they should.' He couldn't work out if she were telling the truth. If not, she was a clever liar. More probably, she wasn't entirely certain, but was making her story up as she went along. Sometimes, Sebastian wished he were dead; sometimes not. That, alas, was human nature. Even vicars lacked consistency.

'Part of the price of being in the public eye,' he said, wondering if being the Vicar of St Teath's in Mallborne was the same as being 'in the public eye'. 'Other people,' he continued, 'have opinions. They seem to believe they have a right to them. And people who are sensitive think they matter.'

'He was certainly sensitive, poor love,' she said, and shook her head. 'He cared. Cared too much, especially about what others thought, or what he thought they thought.' She smiled wistfully, as if to herself. 'He was his own enemy, in that respect. Cared too much. But you can't change human nature. He was always vivid when it came to others. He saw them in Technicolor but he was monochrome himself. So very monochrome. Maybe it was the greyness that killed him. Black and white, even. If he had seen things in colour perhaps he would have survived.'

They both mused. Bognor decided privately that she was slightly deranged, making little or no sense. Greyness and sensitivity suggested something that would not stand up in a court of law, and would cause a jury to have palpitations. A small part of him, however, thought it might just contain a kernel of truth.

'Dorcas was dead,' she said, 'until Saint Peter brought

her back to life. Do you think that can be true? Or was she asleep? Or comatose? I don't think Peter had the gift. Saint or not. I suppose it's possible, though. People must have thought she was dead and that she was then alive, and that Peter had performed the miracle. Sleight of hand, I suppose. Do you think Peter wanted to be thought capable of such a thing? Or was it an embarrassment?'

The doorbell sounded before Bognor could answer. Which he might not have done anyway, not having a plausible response. This felt horribly like religious mania and he was ill-equipped to cope. Mrs Fludd left. Presumably to open the door, and there were indeterminate noises off. Bognor felt he should have strained to catch any verbal exchanges but could not, honestly, be bothered. Eventually, the bishop entered. He was holding Dorcas' hand and looking as near bashful as a bishop can. A coy cleric.

'So you caught the clue,' he said. 'Took your time.'

'I still don't understand.'

Ebenezer smiled at him patronizingly. Only bishops could smile at senior civil servants like that. Bognor felt at once furious and very small. Young even.

'I – we – wanted someone to find out,' said the bishop, 'but not just anyone.'

Bognor frowned. It seemed tricksy to him but then the whole thing seemed contrived. 'Why not just take pills or slit your wrists in the bath?'

'You're thinking it's all a touch melodramatic,' said Ebenezer, 'and maybe it is. Sebastian wanted to go out with a flourish, if not exactly a bang. So maybe we played along too much.'

'I'm not with you,' said Bognor. 'Are you saying it was Sebastian's own wish?' He was groping. It sounded very much as if Ebenezer was suggesting that Dorcas and he had connived in the death. That would make it assisted suicide. A hanging judge would impose a gaol sentence. A liberal might let him off. Or, at least, put them on some form of report.

'In so far as he was capable of making up what you choose to call – in what, if I might say, is a perverse, layman's phraseology "his mind" – then, yes. It was his wish. It was time to go.'

'Who says?'

'We do,' said Dorcas. 'All three of us.'

Bognor did not like this at all. He could see where it was going to end. The bishop was going to pull rank and tell him he had no jurisdiction; that it was a matter for Sebastian and God, with a little help from his friends. Bognor felt increasingly patronized. It was like being back at school, and being told he was too young and inexperienced to have a view. This was a matter for adults, and he was still a child. The bishop and Dorcas were invoking a higher authority. He, however, dealt in more mundane matters. He had to. It was what he was paid for.

'What about the book?' he asked, floundering. 'Did he write a book? Allgood had a story about a book. Used it in his talk. What about the brigadier and the 13th Mobile? Was there a debagging? Did it prey on his mind? Did Brandon's father know something? Did he talk? And what about Vicenza Book, and her mum? What did he really think about them and their sexual antics? What about the harvest supper and Gunther? There are so many unanswered questions . . .'

He stopped in mid-sentence, aware that Dorcas and Ebenezer, the dead man's widow and the dead man's boss, were looking at him with something that veered between contempt and pity. He also realized that while he had a confession of sorts, it was not one that would stand up in court; nor one that would be admitted outside these walls. Dorcas and Ebenezer had helped the vicar on his way. They might have tied the knot; they might have kicked the stool. But it was what the dead man wanted. Correction, it was what Dorcas and Ebenezer said he wanted, and they knew Sebastian better than anyone, certainly far better than any judge and any jury. Bognor knew that he couldn't recommend a prosecution. He knew that if he did such a thing, it would be thrown out. Not only that, but he would be ridiculed and vilified for daring to suggest that he knew better than the dead man's wife and the dead man's bishop, better even than the dead man's God. Even so, he did have a sneaking feeling that this was true and that he was right.

Bognor was not happy.

'I know what you're about to say,' he said. 'You are about to say that Sebastian had lost his faith; that he had lost the capacity to love; that he had lost the capacity to believe. You are going to tell me that it is not my business, nor that of any man on earth. You are going to tell me that this is something which can only be determined in another place. You are about to tell me that my idea of justice and truth is nothing when measured against the eternal verities. You're saying that I and my fellow man are not qualified, that this is best left to something or someone else.'

There was another silence.

Bognor broke it. 'Is that what you're telling me?' he asked, and, even as he asked the question, he knew that he would not receive an answer until he too stood at the pearly gates in which he did not believe. If then. He had an uneasy feeling that St Peter, or his stand-in, would also be shtum.

They both looked at him patiently, sympathetically but condescendingly.

'I'll let myself out,' he said. Neither the bishop nor Dorcas moved. And he left, cheeks stinging but not from the cold.

TWENTY-SEVEN

Simon Bognor never spoke to either ever again. He told Monica what had happened but no one else. She understood and said nothing. Neither Branwell nor Camilla said anything either, though they did not know the whole story.

Everything was tidied away. The verdict was vague. The job was done.

The bishop retired a few months later.

Dorcas left Mallborne a little earlier, and the two went to Cumbria, where they lived together, though they never married.

Dorcas Fludd had met her husband at theological college and it was she who, unsurprisingly, had made the running, and when the race was done, worn the trousers. Bognor guessed as much, but it was good to have Contractor's confirmation. Contractor's researches into the vicar's wife told him little new, but it told him that his waters were right. Or his intuition. The Reverend Sebastian had been one of life's holy fools. His wife was, by comparison, a tungsten-clawed butterfly.

He was reminded of the old saw about the wife who had often contemplated murdering her husband, but never divorce. It had been attributed to Elizabeth Longford, speaking of her maddeningly dotty husband, Frank, the Earl of Longford. Lady Longford was fiercely religious, not the first person one would associate with killing, and not one of life's plagiarists, being of a largely original turn of phrase. It had been a third party who misattributed the remark, which went back a long way, possibly to the first divorce or even the first murder.

Dorcas was a power in Mallborne – in charge of the holy dusters, and the poppy collection, a power in the Women's

Institute and much else besides. She was notionally one of
life's second fiddles but, if one was mixing metaphors, she
had put lead in her husband's pencil. She was light years
away from being an obvious suspect, but Bognor's experience, not least within his own relationship, was that, in
matrimony, all things were possible.

That did not make her a murderer, but Bognor was a
committed believer that when it came to killing people,
wives often dunnit. This had, perforce, to include Dorcas.

A few years later, a book arrived with a printed compliments
slip. It was from a major religious publisher and was by
Ebenezer Lariat. The inscription acknowledged a great debt
to 'my friends Sebastian and Dorcas Fludd'.

'He was only doing his job,' said Monica.

'That's what they all say,' said Bognor. 'It's no excuse.
Pontius Pilate was only doing his job. It's having the courage
not to do the job which separates the men from the beasts.
If everyone just did their job and obeyed orders, we'd be
in an even worse state than we are already.'

Monica knew better than to argue with him. It was a core
belief and important to him. Indeed, he was not rational on
the question of law and order. And orders. Especially orders.
She knew that her husband's first instinct on being given
an order, was to question it. And even though she tended
to disagree with him, it was the main reason she had married
him in the first place.

'I knew Dorcas was there because she found him. But
old Ebb is a bit unexpected.'

'Maybe,' said Monica, 'maybe not.'

'I've always thought bishops were above reproach,' he
said.

'I've always taken a slightly different view of bishops,'
she said. 'Methodists don't have such things, and my instinct
is to think of them as works of the devil. Too much port
and House of Lords. I think your average bishop is a bit of
a dark horse.'

'No such thing as an average bishop,' he said. 'Any more
than an average butler.'

Even so, he had a feeling there was a convention regarding bishops, just as there was with butlers. Trouble was that he couldn't for the life of him remember what it was.

A little later, Bognor read the bishop's obituary in the *Daily Telegraph*. It quoted the Archbishop of Canterbury as saying 'Ebenezer was that rare person – a genuinely good man.'

Dorcas survived him.

So did Simon and Monica.

Simon went to Ebenezer's funeral. He stood at the back and slipped away unnoticed.